ISBN: 9798370121685
ISBN-10: 1477123456

Cover design by: Dreamstime

Printed in the United States of America

To Pauline,
with best
wishes from
Gillian.
X

MARKING TIME

1.

'**C**ome in!'

I have to shout it twice. She's out of breath, I'm gratified to note. It's not just older people who fail after four flights of stairs.

'Sorry I'm a bit late,' she says. 'I don't really do mornings.'

I want to say, A bit late? A bit? I call twenty-five minutes a lot. Do you realise I've not been able to settle to anything because I've been thinking you were coming any minute? There's a double nougat stack of emails to answer and a pile of marking that would frighten a trout.

'That's all right. Have a seat and catch your breath.'

She starts pulling out notes, journal papers. A pair of tights falls on the floor and gets stuffed back into the bag.

'I think I'm just getting a bit overwhelmed. I've got too much material, really.'

'That's ok. It's normal. You can't see the wood for the trees, sort of thing. Have you got any kind of plan? Or do you just want to show me the papers you've got?'

'I thought I'd look at the long-term effects of child sexual abuse – like I said in my email. So I've got the topic. I've got masses of articles on eating disorders, and depression, and psychosis – there doesn't seem to be much of a link there, alcoholism – sorry, alcohol dependency...'

She's needing to do her roots. It's clear that she dyes her own hair from the stark line of new growth in her fringe. Or is this a fashion? I wish I knew.

'You need to remember – I'm sure I've said this in lectures - if you find a higher incidence of childhood sexual abuse in a group of depressed adults, for example, this says nothing about causality. Take any group of adults who have some sort of problem or psychopathology and you'll find higher levels of early abuse. It doesn't imply a causal relationship. Also you have to...'

'But one of these papers says that eating disorders are caused by it.'

'Maybe they're over claiming. I mean, this is what your critical review is about – you've got to think critically about what you read. Just because something is published doesn't mean to say it's good. Some of it'll be good. But quite often if you think about what they're saying there's something wrong. Maybe they've only studied female psychology students, for example. You can't make generalisations from that.'

'Oh. Right.'

She pauses.

'I've a sort of plan,' she goes on.

She dives back into her bag and produces a notepad. She flicks through it slowly. I look out the window at the magpies' nest.

'Here we are.'

I start to read it when there's another knock at the door.

'Yes?'

A youth from third year comes in early for the tutorial. He advances to the table with the chairs set round it.

'Sorry Malcolm. Could you just wait outside a minute? I shouldn't be too long.'

'Sorry.'

The boy smiles and chats to the girl briefly before going out, leaving the door ajar. I hear the word 'club'. Is it a party, or could they possibly be talking about a student political society?

Close the fucking door, I don't actually say. And don't fucking mind me just sitting about here like a turnip while you conduct your social lives. Try fucking working instead.

'This seems ok. You're on the right tracks anyway. Maybe you need to fill in a bit more detail before starting to write it up. You can come...'

The 'phone goes.

'Excuse me,' I say to the girl. 'I'll just see who it is.'

'Dr Lamb?'

The voice sounds like a five-year-old.

'Yes?'

'I missed the lecture last week and just wondered if there were any handouts.'

'May I ask who's speaking?'

'I'm in fourth year.'

There are one hundred and forty students in fourth year.

'Yes, but do you have a name?'

'Oh. Yes. Geraldine.'

'Geraldine. Ok Geraldine. Yes, there were handouts. I can give you them at next week's lecture, though. You don't really need them just now.'

'Are they not on the portal then?'

'No. They're not on the portal. They're not things that can be uploaded. Which is why I brought hard copies to the lecture. But you can get them next week.'

'It's just that I'm not going to be here next week.'

'Oh?'

'I've got to go home. I live up north.'

'I hope there aren't any problems for you?'

'No, it's just cheaper if I go earlier.'

'I see. Well why don't you just drop in and collect them? I'm around all day pretty well. I'm lecturing from two till three but apart from that....'

'Eh...I'm just off to work now.'

'Have you got a lecture?'

'No – my job. I work in Tesco's.'

'In that case I'll put them in an envelope in my pigeonhole across the corridor and you can pick them up in your own good time.'

'I was wondering whether they could be sent out to me. I don't think I'll be back in before the term ends...'

'You just get a pal to pick them up then. Ok? Bye now.'

The girl in the room is fiddling through her papers.

'Sorry about that. And I'm afraid we'll need to stop now. I've got a tutorial group starting this minute. You can email me your plan when you've worked on it a bit more and then we can meet up for a longer discussion.'

Maybe scheduled for the afternoon if you 'do' afternoons. Or will it have to be in the evening? The middle of the night? I show her out and usher in the four who have been waiting outside. Of course there should be six altogether but this is the best attendance yet.

'So. How are we all doing with 'Creativity and Madness'?

2.

When the tutorial is over, I grab my things for the lecture. Outside I bump into Tony, my neighbour in the corridor. He's wearing a suit today. Not a funeral, it transpires, but a meeting with someone from HR.

'You teaching?' he asks

'Fourth year. Last one of the season.'

'Remember not to cheer at the end, then. Anyway, can I drop in later? I need to talk to you.'

'Do you want to give me a clue or is it a nice surprise?'

As if.

'Did you get a letter from HOD?' he goes on.

'No. Is that good or bad?'

'It can only be bad, I think. I've been invited in to 'have a chat'. That's never good is it? I phoned Tessa to ask if she knew what it was about but she was saying nothing. Maybe you're not getting one.'

'God. Something else to worry about. Anyway, sorry – I need to rush. I'll speak to you later. I'll call in after my lecture.'

Like he says, it's never good to 'have a chat'. It might mean demotion, an all-teaching contract. Siberia, even, if they've found a way of doing it. Such chats are always styled 'consultation' but the outcome never reflects the content. Thanks Tony, I think. Back to waking at four in the morning with worry. And at this time of year, not even birdsong.

I trudge along for the ten minutes it takes to get to the hall, carrying my laptop and a briefcase with handouts. I like them to have something to take away – a sort of party bag. I'm buffeted by crowds of students coming towards me who walk three and four abreast taking up the whole pavement. I won't be pushed on to the road so I end up banging into a number of them. A girl's bag gets locked with my briefcase and we do our best to smile. My arms are sore with the weight of everything and I begin to worry about the fight with technology that's ahead. It's raining and I wonder if it's seeping into my lecture notes and washing out the hard copy written in ink. Everyone else seems to be carrying a large polystyrene cup. Have they taken over from phones as the new transitional objects – 'sooky blankets' for grownups? I promise myself a decent coffee after the lecture and positively will the next hour to fly. At last I struggle through the heavy doors of the Maths Building and make my way up to the staff toilet on the third floor. I've just been to the loo but of course need it again. I check my hair in the mirror. The last time I looked I was twenty-six. What happened?

Most of the class have arrived but they're still standing about chatting in groups. They sound excited but I suspect it's not about me or my lecture. The majority haven't noticed I'm there. I look round them boldly – this is a well- practised tactic – and exchange a couple of smiles. There are so many in the class I can't hope to know their faces, far less their names. I tell them at the beginning of the session to say hello if I should be walking past without acknowledging them. This is probably better than the earlier strategy of smiling at everyone under twenty-four in the street.

Bugger. The previous lecturer has undone all the plugs for projecting from laptop to screen. And the connections are numerous and deeply mysterious.

'Dr Lamb.'

My head is still under the table. Perhaps these children have not been taught the importance of eye contact. But I mustn't call them children.

'I just wanted to ask you something about...'

The student tails off.

'It won't take a minute...' she persists.

'Can you come at the end please? I've still got to sort this out and we need to start soon.'

On the wall there's a printed code for the wiring but it bears no relation to what I can see. After five minutes I decide to go with the visualiser instead. Thank goodness for the old overheads. But that previous idiot bastard has also raised the screen. Since this is the last lecture theatre in the university to be modernised, it's manual rather than electronic and I have to jump to pull it down since the loop is high up. I manage to reach it on the third attempt. It's very hot in the room and I'm aware my face is red in spite of wearing summer clothes on a winter's day.

'Ok can we begin now?'

The noise is deafening. It's like a toddlers' party.

'Can we start now?' I bawl.

Two students notice I'm trying to speak and look at me encouragingly.

'Qui-et!' I scream.

They all look at me, surprised.

'Today I want to talk about medical models of psychological abnormality and the problems associated with a category system. The idea that so-called mental diseases can be classified in the same way as physical diseases – into discrete categories so that, for example, you've either got 'schizophrenia' or you haven't. Just like you either have measles or don't have measles.'

I look round the class, trying not to favour the right-hand side. A girl on the second front row is looking intently at me while she spoons soup into her mouth from a bowl.

'I want us to consider whether this is valid, reliable or in any way appropriate and I'll be looking at some of the evidence on these questions today. Just as a first thought: remember – mental patients don't always have the grace to fit into categories that other people devise for them.'

This is my favourite line and I like to get it in early in case I forget. I also worry in case I've already used it with this group. Forgetting is generally a bit of a problem. Sometimes in the middle of a subordinate clause I forget how I started. I've stopped covering up. Now I just ask the class – how did I start that? What was I talking about? I suspect they don't believe me.

I'm nearing the end now. My mouth is dry but the empty glass provided is dirty and the water jug is full of tadpoles.

'So – on the validity question for today - we need to think about the role of social context when diagnoses are being made. As I hope you now realise, diagnostic categories are not derived objectively and psychiatrists are actually making social judgements about a person's behaviour. Just think about someone having auditory hallucinations. As I've said, these are really quite common in the so-called normal population – between ten and fifteen per cent of people hear voices, particularly under certain conditions. But one man's hallucination will bring him a diagnosis and career as a mental patient, while another will be revered for the very same thing. Just think about religious believers.'

I suddenly have the thought that there will be fundamentalists in the class:
'Dear Vice Chancellor, I was deeply offended by Dr Lamb's lecture today. She was very rude about Christians, one of whom I am proud to count myself. I think this is racist and she ought to lose her job.'

'Do you remember Wing,' I go on with a degree of trepidation now, 'the Chief of Police who used to hear god speak to him, telling him what to do? Nobody seemed to think he was abnormal. He kept his job. People looked up to him. There are lots of examples of this sort of thing. So – here's your homework for the vacation. Have a think. Where does religious belief stop and madness begin?'

I'm quite pleased with this ending. By now they're packing up and leaving. I overhear bits of chat.

'... to Andy's tonight? I was speaking to Sarah and she's...'
'...chilli peppers, ordinary peppers, courgettes, ginger...'
As always, there's a small queue of people wanting to

speak to me. They'll tell me about their 'friend' who has psychological problems and I'll do my best. First in line is one of the overseas students. I know because he's excessively polite.

'Can I ask you something about last week's lecture please? Or is it too late now?'

'Of course.'

'On the list which you gave us, about possible signs of child sexual abuse, there was one which said something about ears.'

'Ears?'

'Yes. Some sort of damage or marking on the ears. I was wondering why ears.'

Christ.

'It's one of the erogenous zones,' I hear myself saying, 'and sometimes...'

Pick it up and run, son.

'What does that mean?'

'Erogenous?'

'Yes.'

Is he having me on?

'It's an area of sexual pleasure.'

'Ah.'

He doesn't say anything but takes off his glasses and puts his pen back in his jacket pocket. I'm wondering whether he's going to ask me about sexual pleasure now. The glasses have made me take him seriously; but that's stereotyping for you. You have to be careful. He turns away, ceding to the next in line. And I'm still not sure.

Ten minutes later I'm sitting in the café on the ground floor with a latte in front of me.

3.

He's standing with his back to the wall outside the pub. He's wearing a dark blue wool coat and his shoes are excessively shiny, as with many small men. He's staring in the other direction so I'm able to get a good look.

'Hi!'

He pivots round. It is him. He's not sure whether to shake hands or kiss me on the cheek.

'Shall we?'

He motions to the stairs that lead down to the restaurant. He'd suggested in his text that we might 'have a bowl of soup' in Maximum before going to the pictures. So now I'm sitting in front of a bowl of soup wondering whether the man is so literal in all his dealings. It seems rude to demand more food and at the same time easy to fill up on bread.

His hair is suspiciously dark. When he turns to the waiter I look closely at the sideburns to search for the grey but if he does dye it, he's topped up for the occasion.

'Did Lena get back ok?' he asks.

Our mutual friend now lives in Greece.

'She seems to have. I just got a text. It's a wonder she got up in time to catch the plane though.'

'I don't know what would have happened if we hadn't taken her home.'

He had come with me, holding her other arm. Once inside, he refused to go into the bedroom she shared with her partner, which seemed quaint on his part but somehow a bit appealing. Her bed was messed – blood on the sheets which were half on the floor. I'd held her shoulders positioning her to fall on to the bed.

She made a move to kiss me on the lips.

'Night Lena,' I said, pushing her on the bed.

'So you've just got your mother?' he's saying.

'Mm. My father died a few years ago,' I go on. 'My mother's getting old now.'

'Is she in a Home?'

I nod.

'Just recently – a few months ago,' I go on, 'We're still emptying the house and all that.'

'You're lucky, still having her.'

'I dare say.'

'That sounds a bit half-hearted.'

'Things have always been a bit difficult between her and me.'

'Yes but she's still your Mum.'

'Not all mothers and daughters get on you know.'

'I was very close to my Mum. Have I told you about when she died?'

He hasn't. On the other hand, at Lena's house he had talked about his father's death for some time.

'She'd been taken into hospital,' he starts now. 'It was awful. She was only supposed to be in for a couple of days while they stabilised her blood sugar. Then they got the vomiting bug on the ward and that brought her down and then she got another infection and...'

He goes on for a full three minutes I swear, and three minutes is a long time for one person in a conversation.

'Which hospital?' I interrupt. I want to hear my own voice. I want to be sure I'm still there.

He continues in the litany, culminating in a final scene where the family are gathered round the bed. In the meantime I'm starving. My soup is cold but it's rude at the best of times to continue eating when someone is talking to you.

'So you see, think yourself lucky still having your Mum.'

'I'm not saying I won't be sad when she goes but she was

always very critical of me, you know.'

'But you'll miss her.'

'Of course. In a way.'

'Come on. You'll be devastated. It's the worst thing in the world losing your Mum.'

'No it's not. I can think of worse things.'

'Like what?'

'Like losing a child.'

This was desperate stuff.

'I don't have children,' he says.

'But you do have an imagination.'

'I just know it's the worst thing that's ever happened to me and I think it will be the same for you.'

'Worse than when your wife left you?'

'Yes and that was hard. But not as hard. And I think you would find the same.'

'I don't think I will, to be honest. And I don't think you can tell me how I'll feel. You don't know me.'

The waiter arrives, hoping to take away our plates.

'Are you both finished?'

'We've hardly started,' I say, reaching out for more bread.

Dyed hair man takes the chance to grab my hand.

'You'll see. You'll see.'

'My boots are hurting. And we're going to be late for the film.'

He helps me into my coat. I've got a bit of bread stuck up the sleeve. And I bet he does dye his bloody hair.

4.

I'm writing feedback on an essay, suggesting amongst other things that the student give it a title. I want to say 'Would you like to go through life without a name?' But this is excessive, as it would be to suggest that leaving out references is a criminal offence. Then I tackle the emails. "Hey Madeleine..." one starts. At the end there's a kiss. I've never met this student but now she's my best friend.

'Madeleine? Hello how are you?'

The HOD's secretary is on the phone: "Just a little chat... when suit... nothing to worry about. No, don't know what it's about."

This is surely a contradiction.

'Hi Tony'.

I'm straight into his office.

'Your little chat with the HOD? I meant to see you about it,' I say. 'Sorry. Have you had it yet? I'm being lined up for one too.'

He's sitting behind a structure formed of a desk and two tables. He couldn't make it more obvious unless he worked inside the cupboard.

'No,' he says, 'but Dick has. Remember the re-grading exercise last summer? It seems they want to demote some of us to 'university teachers.' Of course they don't use 'downgrade' and they're very keen to point out that the salary scales are the same. They claim that there are 'no implications'. It's the thin edge of the wedge. I would guess there might even be redundancies.'

'God.'

I'm feeling queasy.

'Dick's told HOD to stuff it and now he's gone to the Union. It's blindingly obvious that we'd get dumped with more teaching and have even less time for research. They just don't admit that teaching is a punishment. In the meantime those other buggers would swan off on the Dent Travel Fund and have even less to do with students. Some of them wouldn't know a student if they were hit with one.'

'At least we're prepared now,' I suggest. 'Forewarned and all that. Mind you, once Management have made up their minds...'

'That little bugger Mason had it in for us from the beginning. "Deadwood", he called us, remember? These new bastards always do it. My mate Mike in Biology's been leaned on every time there's been an offer on. Voluntary redundancy, early retirement, you name it.'

'He's done well to survive,' I suggest.

'He's a stubborn bastard, that's why. The joke is, when they put on that bash for long service – you know, finger food, warm wine and the Vice Chancellor for five minutes - they actually leant on him to go along and pick up his tasteful little print of the university. We reckoned that each one cost the university £30. That's £1 for each year of service. Pretty good, eh?'

'I look forward to it. Shit.'

I can hear my mobile going off next door. When I reach it, I recognise a voice from the Home.

'Hello. Is that Dr Lamb? Madeleine Lamb.'

'Yes?'

'I don't want you to be alarmed but this is Pamela from Fairweather Care Home. We were trying to get hold of your brother but he wasn't answering. It's about your mother.'

5.

'She's not here yet.'

I'm standing at Reception in the hospital. The receiving nurse is looking down at the form. I could be a chimpanzee for all she knew.

'What did you say her name was again?'

I tell her.

'What was the date of birth?'

I tell her again.

'No, I think the ambulance is still on its way,' she decides. 'They'll come in at the back entrance so if you just take a seat we'll let you know when she's arrived.'

There's one empty space left, next to a girl who's crying. She seems to be on her own and I want to speak to her but worry that it's an intrusion. The receptionist announces my name. I manage to locate the cubicle she sends me to but inside there's a young man. I back out and start to call on my mother, mindful that she's a bit deaf. Since that fails, I finally retrace my steps, tell the receptionist what's happened and sit down again.

When eventually I am summoned to the right place, my mother is lying back on the bed looking older than she's ever done, with her teeth out and her face concave. The blanket fails to cover her so that her mottled legs and puffy ankles stick out. I'm frightened in case I see more. But she sparkles when she sees me.

'It's you Madeleine. That was good of you to come.'

What's good is that she recognises me.

'Not at all. How do you feel?'

'I'm fine thank you. How are you?'

'You were brought here in an ambulance so you can't be completely fine.'

'Was I? When?'

'Just now. You've just arrived.'

'Where am I?'

'You're in hospital.'

'Why am I here?'

'You're not well.'

'I feel fine. What's this?'

She pulls at the hospital band on her wrist.

'My goodness a plastic watch,' she says.

She's wired up and a machine next to the bed is following the signs of her life. I'm wondering what to do if one of the signals were to stop when a doctor comes in and shakes my mother's hand. She's charmed.

'How do you do,' she says enunciating clearly in her best voice.

She'll be offering cups of tea at her own funeral. The pair of them proceed to a patchwork conversation about her medical history.

'No – I've never had any trouble with my heart,' she's saying.

She always wonders what some families do to deserve so much illness. She's never ill herself. Angina, angioplasty? No, she's saying. I, however, tell the doctor she has amnesia because she's had the lot.

'I've been very lucky with illness you know,' she's still insisting when I leave before any of her clothes are removed.

Back at the waiting room my brother has arrived and in two minutes we're making jokes. He's always resolved problems into jokes which is fine really, but I'm different. Eventually we're called back in to hear the verdict. My mother's face shines to see him.

'Oh Miles!'

It's one of the few times I've been able to imagine her with a lover. I wave my arms.

'I'm here too.'

When we go, she breathes to him alone:

'Bye bye Miles. Bye bye thank you.'

I hit him when we get outside and hope that the nurses don't see.

I drive home on my own with a bag of her smelly clothes stuck on the seat beside me. You're always living with the smell of others, which is good sometimes. Good being twenty and your face in the pillow in the early morning after your lover has gone. Breathing in, lingering, till the scent has disappeared and you have to accept that they're no longer there.

I think of all the scents I've loved – pine trees wafted by the wind; salt sea and seaweed; my father's pipe smoke. Even the biscuit smell from our dog's ears. If I could just have them now, for a while. If only we could put days in the bank to draw on in the future.

There's a photograph of her and my father before they were married. In it they're standing on rocks by the beach wearing their swimsuits. That's the most I ever saw of their bodies. My father has said something to make her laugh and she has put her hand up to cover her mouth but you can see the mirth in her eyes.

They took us back on holiday to this place throughout our childhood so that now, looking back, I can measure how I fared with her each year. Mostly it was fine. Only one time stands out:

'Don't forget the paper as well today,' she said, putting money in my hand.

I was seven and setting out for the morning rolls. The shop owner was old and blind. He kept a parrot which never talked any sense but amused us all the same. I was on my own and felt favoured but of course Miles didn't even notice. He wasn't keeping score, unlike me. In the shop I could look at the toy I'd been wanting. It was beyond the reach of my pocket money, though. There on the lower shelf it sat: a plastic beach set, with a little spade and shapes that you filled with sand to make shells and fish and mermaids. I would have put them round my castles.

'Here you are.'

The old man handed me the things.

'I guess you're still looking at your set?'

I nodded. As if he could see.

'You'll need to save.'

'I don't think I've time. We go home next week.'

'What's that?'

A stranger had come in. He didn't show any surprise to be served by a blind person.

'How much is it?'

And so he bought it for me. I never saw him again. I went home without the change because I'd lost it and then told them that a stranger had bought the toy. When my mother was angry with me, it started at her lips before she even spoke. But it was the coldness rather than her words that cut me and I longed to make up and have her love me again because I didn't know whether being cast out would ever end.

'You can stay in this afternoon,' she said. 'We don't tell lies in this family.'

I never saw the toy again.

It's a glass of wine when I get home. I put her washing in the machine right away even though the noise will keep me awake. There are three messages on the phone.

'Hi Maddie. It's Tony. I just wanted to ask how your mother is. Hope things are all right. If you're in tomorrow I'll tell you about one of your students who was looking for you. Oh... and his nibs was up at your door too.'

HOD. Damn. And in person.

'Maddie. It's Marcia. Just trying to sort out a meeting for the Group. No worries. Speak soon.'

She's so cheerful in spite of her husband.

'Hello Madeleine. I'm sorry you had to rush off the other night. I enjoyed the evening very much. I was wondering if you

would be free next Saturday. I've got a couple of tickets for...'
    I put the phone down. It's the man who dyes his hair.

6.

'**R**osie. Hello. Come in.'

She's small and dark haired. I can only work with two attributes, so all the students fall into one of a very few categories.

'I believe you wanted to talk to me about your project?'

'Yes. Thanks for seeing me. I wasn't sure who to speak to.'

'Who's your supervisor then? Why aren't you seeing them if I may ask?'

She named the HOD.

'Are you worried about it? Is it not going very well?'

She's quiet.

'Do you not feel you can talk to him about it then?'

She looks down but I can see that there are tears in her eyes.

'I'm sorry. I'm really sorry,' she says.

'You don't need to worry about that.'

I pass her a box of tissues which are always to the ready.

'Here. Now don't feel bad. You're not the first student to have cried in this room. I can cry myself too, you know.'

She tries to smile but this makes it worse and reminds me how upsetting kindness is when you're down.

'Look. Just take your time. You can tell me what's wrong and I'll try to sort it.'

'I don't want anyone to know.'

'If you mean you don't want anyone other than me to know, then that may be ok, but I can't guarantee it, to be honest. And if it's something that your Advisor needs to know, something that is affecting your ability to cope here, I would try to convince you to let me tell him or her.'

'It's not that. I just don't want the other students knowing.'

'There's no need for them to know anything you don't tell them yourself. And as for the other staff... well, maybe you'll want to tell the Course Tutor if you're going to be late handing your project in...but I don't know. I don't know what the problem is.'

'Could I not change my supervisor?'

'I'm not sure I could do that without a reason, I'm afraid.'

Rosie says nothing.

'It's just that it's not usual at this time of year. If the supervisor and student don't get on, it's usually clear at the beginning of term. Have you actually been having meetings with him? Or is that the problem – is he not available? I know he's away a lot.'

'We've met several times,' she says. 'It's not that. I don't feel comfortable with him. I just want to change.'

'I would need to discuss it with him too, you know. It wouldn't be...'

'Can you not just take me on yourself?' she asks.

'But he would notice, Rosie. Anyway, it wouldn't be fair to do that. I wouldn't like it if someone poached one of my students.'

She gives a small smile.

'I suppose not. So what would you have to say to him?'

'At the moment I'm not sure. It would be good to be able to present him with something... some reason.'

'I don't like the area.'

'Cog neuro?'

'Yes.'

'I don't think that's going to work as a reason. You must have chosen him as a supervisor in the first place so you would have known what you were getting in to. I don't mean to be unsympathetic – I'm just trying to understand. Is it because you're not collecting your own data? I know that students can't really do their own experiments in that area. Are you going to be working on his data?'

'That's mostly it.'

'Right. But you know, other staff do the same thing – have their students work on data they provide. I would really be a bit reluctant to make that argument too.'

'He's a bit creepy.'

'Creepy? How do you mean?'

'I think he fancies me.'

'What? What makes you think that? Look, maybe you don't want to tell me and that's ok. But I'll certainly not broadcast it.'

'I don't really want to go into it.'

She blows her nose.

'This is difficult Rosie. I do want to help and I can see that you would want to change supervisor. I'm a bit puzzled though. Between you and me, he really doesn't have a reputation for going after students. We usually know the sexual predators - though of course I shouldn't be telling you this. I'm not saying you're not telling the truth though. Well, we'll have to do something about it. I mean 'we the staff' – not you. It's not your responsibility for sorting it out. In the meantime, just to keep things going, I wonder if I could get hold of some of his data for you to be working on.'

'I've got some data.'

'Oh right. So did he pass on some of his?'

'It's my own. I did the experiment myself.'

'The new scanner stuff - do you mean the new MRI study?'

'Yes.'

'You were a subject for it? I should say 'participant'.'

The term 'subject' had been replaced.

'Gosh. I didn't know he'd gone through Ethics for it.'

I sat on the Ethics Committee and was sure his application hadn't yet been approved.

'I don't know about that.'

'What do you mean? Did you not fill in a consent form?

'No.'

'Did you get an information sheet? About the purpose of the experiment, contraindications and so on?'

'No.'

'Can I be quite clear here? Did you get put in an MRI scanner without getting any information about the procedure or filling in a consent form?'

'He said it was ok. He said there weren't any risks – that it was known to be very safe.'

'I see. Right. Ok. Look, I'm sorry but I am going to have to talk to some other people about this. They will regard it as confidential too so it won't be spread about. But I can't just deal with this on my own. I think there's a problem with what he's done and it's a bit difficult knowing at the moment how to deal with it. Not least because he's Head of Department.'

'What should I do?'

She starts to cry again.

'Rosie, I'll get on to this right away. I would like you to leave it with me but come and see me tomorrow afternoon. Have you got someone at home? Are you in hall or a flat or what?'

'I'm in a flat but I'm on my own – my last flatmate gave up university and I've just got a new one. She's moving in after Christmas.'

'Have you got a friend who could keep you company this evening? I'm just a bit worried about your being so upset.'

'I suppose I could ask Daisy.'

'Will you do that please? And come and see me tomorrow afternoon. Let's see when we're both free.'

What a stupid little bugger Mason is. What an ass. Does he not realise the limits of professorial impunity?

7.

'Hello Madeleine. Have a seat.'

It's lower than his. Mason is not an idiot in terms of designing his office.

'Do you know why I've asked you to come?'

'I assumed you would tell me.'

'I thought maybe you'd have talked to one of the others. Tony, for example.'

He's fishing but I'm not going to shop Tony.

'It doesn't really matter, does it?' I say. 'You can tell me now.'

'Yes. Well, I've been looking at your record of publications and grant money for the last few years...we've been looking. That is, the Management Group.'

'Yes?'

'It's not as strong as we would like, I'm afraid. You're as aware as I am that your duties here encompass not only teaching and administration but research as well.'

'Indeed I am aware and the fact is that I have done a great deal of research. I've had several grants as you know. I've also supervised several PhD students and examined PhDs elsewhere.'

'Yes, but not to the same extent as some other members of staff.'

'Who are you thinking of?'

'It would be wrong of me to name names but I think you know the people I mean.'

'You tell me. If you're making comparisons with other people I need to know who you're comparing me with.'

'Madeleine, are you not making this a little more difficult

than necessary? I can point to people who have got three or four good publications a year and hold several grants. People who have been doing this for years too.'

'And I can tell you that these are people who've been given very little teaching and no administration.'

'That's just not true.'

'It's largely true, I think you'll find. There are some people in this Department who give only six lectures a year.'

'That is not their total teaching. They are all doing a lot of research supervision and that is teaching. So is supervising the PhDs that they have.'

'Yes, their PhDs do their undergraduate supervision and write their papers for them.'

'You have no reason to say that. I don't see that we'll get anywhere if you are just going to be objectionable.'

His face and hair are going grey. He looks like an old rat.

'Ok you think I'm being objectionable. Why don't you just tell me what this is all about? As far as I'm concerned, all you've done is say negative things about me so far, to no purpose.'

HOD leans towards me, shortening the distance between us. I can see his nose hairs now.

'Madeleine, the Department does appreciate what you do here. I appreciate what you do here. You do a wonderful job.'

He pauses.

'The students love you. I know that. And I don't know what we'd do without you.'

'Can I have that in writing?'

'What's that?'

He pretends not to hear.

'Just joking,' I say. 'So why am I here now? Why are you saying all this about not having enough publications?'

'We think that what you contribute to the Department would be better represented by a slightly different job title. Perhaps 'Senior Lecturer' isn't quite right. Perhaps...'

'What?'

'What do you mean, what?'

'What do *you* mean? What's wrong with 'Senior Lecturer'? It's been all right up till now.'

I'm having a flashback to a dream that has followed me all day. A dream of finding my mother wandering about an old asylum which has closed down. She's wearing a shift nightdress and is picking her way over discarded canisters, bottles, cannulas, needles, drips. When she sees me, she grabs hold of my arm and my last memory is of staring at her long nails sticking into my flesh, drawing blood.

'Your situation is more compatible, we have decided, with a designation of 'University Teacher'. Now, you needn't have any worries at all about this. It means nothing.'

'So why do you suggest it?'

'The salary's the same. It's not a demotion. In fact, it could open up the way to promotion, along a different track. You could eventually become a Professor of Teaching.'

'Don't tell me there's not a loss of status.'

'Only if you don't value the teaching aspect of your job.'

'You know that I do. But I also value my research. I assume this new title would mean I only teach.'

'That brings me to another point. Your research is too...well... applied.'

'And what's wrong with that?'

'It's not just me. The assessment of the university is based on pure research...'

'Are you saying that in the grand scheme of things my research on children's welfare is less important than your research on the caudate nucleus?'

'We all know what's good research and what isn't.'

'I think you're missing my point.'

'Which is?'

'If you can't see what I'm saying I'm not sure I can explain it.'

This dream about my mother. It must be because she's in hospital. The shift she wears too.

'While we're talking about children's welfare, I'd like to

bring up the matter of one of your project students,' I go on.

'I can't quite see the link frankly but if you don't mind, I'd rather finish our conversation first.'

'I thought we had finished. You invited me to change my designation. I am declining. Thank you.'

'You realise that I'll have to go to Human Resources and take advice?'

'Then I'm afraid it looks as if I'll be speaking to the Union. So be it. Can we talk about your project student now?'

'Which one?'

'Rosie.'

'Ah, Rosie. What about her?'

'MRI scan?'

'What about it?'

'You put her through the scanner?'

'Only because she was so keen.'

'Keenness has never been a criterion. There are people keen to have their limbs amputated.'

'I think you're straying into territory where you're not wanted.'

'Well I can believe that.'

His phone rings. He turns his back to me while he answers.

'No, it's all right. I'll be there in a minute. I've got someone with me but we've just finished.

'I'm so sorry Madeleine. I'm needed elsewhere. Why don't you just have a good think about your position? Bear everything in mind. I mean everything. Then we can talk again and I believe we might be able to negotiate something.'

I bang my knee on his desk when I get up. He remains standing till I leave the room.

8.

The Home is next to a busy road. A noticeboard in the hallway says: 'Today is Friday. It is cold and windy.' It's none of these. There's a strong chemical smell that's marginally better than what it's masking. My mother is in the dining room where dinner is being served exceptionally early, as always.

She looks so delighted that I imagine she knows me. She's scarcely coping with the fork so I take it from her and start to pick up small bits of food. I notice her wedding ring has disappeared. When I feed her, I realise that I'm opening my own mouth, like all mothers do with their babies.

'You look well,' I say. 'Do you feel well?'

'I feel fine dear. I'm so pleased to see you.'

Some food falls out of her mouth.

'Good. And do you know who I am?'

'Yes.'

'Do you remember my name?'

I'm not often this cruel.

'Yes.'

'What is it?'

'What's what?'

'My name. What's my name. I'm your daughter, you know.'

'Daughter? I'm not! Am I?'

'No, you're not my daughter. I'm your daughter. You've got two children, a boy and a girl. And I'm your girl. We're Miles and....?'

She thinks hard.

'Aunty...,' she starts.

Maybe she's remembering that I am indeed an aunt. Aunty Madeleine.

'Yes?'

She looks around and notices the piano.

'Aunty Piano.'

'You daftie. I'm Madeleine. Your daughter, Madeleine.'

'That's right dear.'

She was always right.

'Isn't that nice,' she says, 'you can see all the way down to the harbour.'

'It does look at bit like a harbour.'

The lights of the town twinkle far away in the valley.

'There aren't any people though.'

'It's too far away for you to see them.'

'That's useful for you to know where you are,' she says.

'When they come in it's always the same,' says the woman opposite.

This woman's wearing a lot of jewellery for someone who can't dress herself.

'You mean, when people come into the Home?' I say to her.

'When they pick up the rubbish and the chances are due. You see they're here and that's the end of it but they don't tell you.'

She pushes out her top teeth with her tongue and stares at me.

'I guess so.'

It's very hot in the room. For a brief silly moment I wonder if she's talking about the angel of death but that's just fanciful. I should be past that. A carer comes over to cajole the woman into eating.

'Come on now. You be good. There'll be no video for you tonight if you don't eat your dinner.'

In a room off the corridor on my way out a bed-ridden voice is calling for help.

As children Miles and I would stay at our aunt's thatched cottage in the country. It hadn't yet been 'improved', so the light came from a paraffin lamp and the only tap in the house drew from a stream which ran outside. A spider came through once, which made us careful. At night we would lie in the top bunks, talking till we were scolded for a third time but happy in the certainty that there would be rabbits outside on the grass in the morning.

In the day we would annoy water spiders in the stream and look for fairy rings in the woods. We ran over the bridge past the witch's house to the gate that led to a T-shaped wood and the hills beyond. The dog came until it got fed up or anxious and went home on its own. We pretended to be film stars posing amongst the gorse bushes. There was no notion of time or future.

My aunt was tall and glamorous. When she got older and put on weight round the middle she looked like a robin with her long, slim legs. She wore strong lipstick and put garlic in her spaghetti while my mother would leave it out. She had been considered the black sheep of the family but only for smoking and once driving a car into the wall. All of this made her immensely attractive. We weren't aware of her bad marriage.

'Let's hear it again.'

She was laughing at something I'd said. It was nice that she passed on her giggle to her daughter. I wish I could remember what had amused her, me standing there, aged four, in pyjamas in the darkening room with its low ceiling. I can still see the hurt look on my cousin's face and trace her jealousy back to that moment. But at the time it was wonderful to be the centre of someone's attention.

She was so proud of my job when I got it, my aunt. I really believe she was. Whereas for my mother I was just a cipher. 'My daughter, the university lecturer.' It was an instant finesse. What I had learned or taught or what I did with my day actually meant nothing to her.

Years later my aunt was the head matron in a boys'

boarding school – a nominal but powerful role - by virtue of being the head teacher's wife.

'Milly, will you do the potatoes now?' she would ask cook.

She had staff to manage, you see, and everything seemed to be carried out on an industrial scale. The potatoes, for example, had to be peeled in a large machine like a cement mixer.

'I'll check we have enough jam for tomorrow,' she'd say.

And she would go off to the huge pantry, look along the lines of tins on the shelves. Not tins as I knew them, but tins for giants. Even the jam came in tins. Then she and I might go upstairs to their private flat to have a smoke. We were co-conspirators in many ways.

'Milly's all right but she'll be leaving soon you know,' she said on one of these occasions.

'Why? She's been here for years.'

'Don't you say this to a soul. Promise now.'

Of course I promised.

'She's pregnant.'

'How could she be? She doesn't have a boyfriend, does she?'

'She's been with someone. I tried to get it out of her but she won't say.'

'What a shame. When does she have to go?'

'About four weeks and it'll start to show. We can't have her around the boys. I just hope nothing ever gets back to the parents. Don't you be saying anything about it.'

'Does Elaine not know?'

I thought she might have told her daughter.

'I'm not sure I can trust her, to be honest. She's quite close to Milly. Although I don't think she knows about this development yet.'

'I won't say but is it not a bit funny that I know and...? Anyway, what'll happen to Milly?'

'She'll have it adopted.'

'Why?'

'She can't afford to look after it herself.'

'She's got parents. Won't they help?'

'She doesn't want them to know.'

I could see this. But what a price.

'Poor thing. Where will the baby go? I mean, is it Social Work that'll do it?'

'I've got a friend – you know Edith – she does voluntary work with…'

She named some charity.

'She'll make sure some nice family is found.'

'But it's not up to her. Surely?'

'Not in theory but she's got a lot of influence and…'

'That's awful. How come a friend of yours will know where Milly's baby goes and poor Milly won't know herself? That's not fair.'

'She should have thought of that earlier.'

9.

I'm at work the day after Rosie misses her appointment. 'Madeleine!'

It's the phone and I'm supposed to guess who it is. I hate this.

'It's Steven,' he finally says when I can't fill the silence. The Chief Advisor.

'Sorry Steven. I just wasn't expecting you and your voice is quite like a few others…'

'Madeleine. How can you say that? Moi? Like anyone else?'

'Fraid so chum. Anyway, what can I do for you?'

'I've been trying to tell you for years.'

'I mean now. I mean – tell me your business - Jesus Christ you're annoying.'

'It's about one of your students,' he explains.

'Yes. Which one out of the eleven hundred might that be then?'

'Rosie Chapman.'

'Rosie? What is it? I was about to contact her. She was due to come for a meeting with me yesterday and didn't show.'

'Well, good reason. She's in hospital.'

'Hospital? God. What it is? I hope it's not anything bad.'

'I'm afraid I can't tell you dear girl. I don't know myself.'

'So…?'

'Her mother phoned. They got me involved because she's going to miss some deadline – not one of yours – it's one of her other subjects. But I had express instructions to let you know what was going on.'

'Her mother just said hospital and didn't say what?'

'Correct, and I think you're expected to visit. I don't know how long she's in for but it must be more than a couple of days. I don't know. They wouldn't ask you to go otherwise, would they? Can you do it?'

'I'll make time. I've been worrying about her.'

'Really? Do say.'

'Maybe another day. There's no need to tell you anything now. In fact…'

'So does that mean we get to meet up? What about a drink after work?'

'And what does Madame Russell say about that?'

'Madame Russell knows that occasionally I have a drink with other women. She doesn't mind at all.'

'I hope she sees other men for a drink then.'

'She's entitled to.'

'Look, we can email. Just tell me what hospital she's in please.'

And so I'm in a hospital again, a different one this time, making my way up to Obstetrics and Gynaecology on floor 10. You would expect some sort of quietness there, out of deference to the lost babies, the radium packs in the womb and all such things but instead it's a fairground. I spot Rosie in the corner bed. She has no other visitor. Her eyes are shut and she's frowning in her sleep. I sit on the plastic chair near the end of her bed and wait.

'She came in last night.'

This is the woman in the next bed.

'Right. Thanks.'

'She's just being monitored at the moment. She was supposed to be getting a scan but there's some problem with staff or the machine or something. She's going to be all right but they don't know about the baby yet.'

'I see.'

'You're not a big sister, are you?' she goes on. 'You seem a bit old for that. But you can't be her mother…?'

She holds on to her side and pulls herself up.

'No. I'm just a friend.'

'I didn't think so. I think it was her mother that brought her in last night but I didn't really see. They put the screens round.'

I look at Rosie still sleeping, her breathing soft and quick. I don't want to waken her and I don't want to leave either.

'I'm being investigated myself,' the neighbour goes on. 'I'm Margaret, by the way.'

'Madeleine. Hello.'

'That's a nice name. It's quite unusual, isn't it? Mine's so ordinary. Still – I'm used to it. They don't know what's happening with me. I've got some sort of mass round my ovary – it sticks out. Would you like to see it?'

'Thanks. I don't think so. I'm a bit squeamish.'

Rosie stirs and turns over.

'There. She's wakening up. Why don't you speak to her? She'll waken up.'

I take my chair to the other side of the bed, away from Margaret.

Rosie's eyes are open.

'Hi Rosie.'

She smiles.

'Hello Dr Lamb. Did you hear then?'

'The Chief Advisor got the message to me. How are you?'

'It's painful.'

'I'm sorry.'

'Do you know then?' she asks.

'What's wrong? Just what Margaret over there said, I'm afraid. A baby.'

Rosie rolls her eyes.

'I was pregnant. I am pregnant. I might be losing it though.'

'I'm sorry Rosie. Are you sure?'

'They can't tell for certain because they haven't got a machine free yet to do a scan but the nurse thinks it's probably too late. I've had so much bleeding. The doctor isn't saying that though – she said that you could have bleeding – even quite a lot – and the baby will still be all right.'

'I wouldn't know. I'm a bit useless as far as that's concerned, I'm afraid. It's very upsetting.'

'It's all right. I wasn't sure to begin with myself. When I first found out I was pretty horrified. I'm ashamed to say that now. I even wonder if I'm being punished for thinking it.'

'That's not right. I know that at least. It doesn't work like that, Rosie, and don't you think that way. That's how they thought hundreds of years ago. Miscarriages are very common, I believe. Anyway, you've not lost the baby yet. It could still be ok.'

'I just feel that I have. There was so much blood last night and it was old blood, you know, dark, which the nurse says is a bad thing.'

'So what are they going to do, apart from the scan?'

'They've done hormone tests and it's not like I've got some hormone deficiency or anything that makes the baby rejected. Where they can do something about it. They say that technically I'm still pregnant, though. That's from the blood tests. All I can do is wait.'

Margaret calls over.

'Are you feeling any better pet?'

'A bit better than last night thanks.'

'That's nice your friend could come in. Have you got your mother coming in again?'

'She's coming tonight.'

'And what about your husband? Has he been yet?'

Rosie looks at me.

'Sorry Margaret,' I say. 'I'm actually Rosie's tutor and we're just going to have a talk about work things.'

'Oh. Right then. I'll catch up later.'

'I don't even have a boyfriend,' Rosie goes on, quietly.

She seems to be apologising.

'That doesn't mean anything now,' I say. 'I know it did once... maybe it does to your mother? I don't know. Of course, it would be nice if you had some support from the baby's father but...'

'I'm not even sure who the father is.'

'Oh Rosie.'

I nearly hug her.

'I know it's awful. It's stupid. But...' She tails off.

'What had you planned to do? Would you want to stay on at university? Or would you take a year out?'

'My mum would have looked after it.'

It. 'It' is all things and anything. For one woman it's 'tissue'; for another, it's an embryo. I think I would call it 'my baby', but what do I know?

'And when you finish university? Do you want to go on in Psychology and become a professional psychologist?'

'You'll laugh at me. I was just thinking yesterday afternoon what I wanted to be most of all.'

A smile comes to her face.

'What's that?'

'A time traveller. I've been reading about quantum physics...'

She starts to giggle.

'They're quite close to creating a sort of time machine...'

Now she's talking about time travel and how she would like to be a time traveller and her arms are outstretched and she's illustrating what she's saying by crooking the index and middle finger of each hand like you do when casting rabbit-ear shadows on the wall. And I'm giggling too, at the same time as wondering whether she's lost a bit of her reason.

Then it comes to me.

'Rosie. When exactly did you go through the scanner? I mean, the MRI in the Psychology Department. With Professor Mason?'

10.

'Richard. Fancy seeing you here.'
I bump into him when I'm leaving the hospital. He's wearing a tweed jacket with dull pink cord trousers. He's just visiting a friend.

'Do you know Keith? Keith Watson?'

Kidney problems, he goes on to explain.

'Come and have a coffee,' he suggests.

We go to the nearest café. Old fashioned, with booths for hiding and having affairs in. Adverts for ice cream cones and certificates of merit on the wall. A university practically.

'Richard, you'll know about this. Magnetic resonance imaging. You know how we've got the new scanner?'

'I do indeed. The whole university knows. I think your Centre has eaten up the whole development budget for the next five years.'

'Do you know about contra-indications for being scanned?'

'Sure. The 'real' ethics committee had to find out all this stuff before applications started coming through.'

He's referring to the fact that he's on the University Ethics Committee, and not the minor one I'm on. As rank pulling goes, it's pathetic.

'Good. I mean I'm glad you know about it.'

'Why are you asking?'

'I've been wondering how safe it is. Not that I'll ever be in that building but we've all been making jokes about not wearing earrings or cufflinks when we pass by. What are the specific problems, then?'

'Apart from it blowing up?'

'Does it?'

'Only when they're installing or removing it. So yours is past the point of greatest danger now. You needn't worry for another seven or eight years I reckon.'

'What are the other dangers? And the contra-indications?'

'Epilepsy. Pregnancy. Plus lots related to the magnet reacting with metal or foreign bodies in the person being scanned. Say they've got a pacemaker or something like that. The magnet creates a charge in the metal and it's like being burned and torn from the inside. The biggest problem is with unsuspected sources of metal. There was someone with breast implants which they thought was fine because they were silicone, but then it turned out that there was a metal identification chip. Her breast was fried.'

People round about us are eating all day breakfasts.

'That isn't funny,' I tell him.

Richard is grinning.

'Sorry. It's nerves,' he says. 'You also have to be careful about the direct effects on the muscles, especially the myocardium which is just a muscle as you know.'

He's in lecture mode, going on about tissue heating and thermoregulatory responses.

'Probably the biggest thing is that you have to be careful not to introduce a metal source into the room. Otherwise it's down the tube at 150 miles an hour. Patients can get lacerated by hairpins.'

He's enjoying this.

'Tell me more about pregnancy,' I ask. 'I imagine it's not a great idea to do an MRI on pregnant women. But then some people think that pregnant woman shouldn't eat sliced bread.'

'It's the noise - the vibrations affecting the foetus. No one will scan pregnant women.'

'What if they don't know? The woman herself might not

know.'

'Medical centres will do a test but of course they can't do that in your place, can they, since you're not medics and it's just research?' he asks.

'What sort of damage is there? Is the foetus harmed directly or what?' Could it cause a miscarriage, say?'

'Not enough data. You have to suspect it's possible, though. Why all these questions?'

'Just that in our place a lot of the participants are likely to be female students. All our students have to take part in a certain number of staff experiments. What would happen if, just supposing, someone went ahead and scanned a student without checking for pregnancy?'

'A total no no. Kicked out of the Brownies. A criminal offence, in my view. But you're not telling me…?

'I'm not telling you anything.'

'Just wondering. Thank goodness. Anyway, what have you been up to?'

'Since I last saw you…when was that anyway? Was it as long ago as the summer?'

'I think so.'

'I was in Crete for a couple of weeks – you know, visiting Lena. Of course you don't know Lena. Let me tell you about something else though. I've just given blood. You went on at me about it once. Do you remember? Anyway, I've done it now so you don't need to nag any more.'

'That's great.'

I wait for him to ask me about it, listen to my bad stories about blood backing up the arm. But he's thinking.

'I wonder when it was that I last gave blood. It was years ago. It must have been when I was in Turkey. The time of the earthquake. Do you remember?'

He'd been on a field trip and got caught up. I've heard the story from him before. He tells me it all again and my own little experience fades away.

'I need to go now Richard. Sorry,' I eventually interrupt

him.

'Are you going home now? I could give you a lift.'

'No. But thanks. I think I'll go back to the Department for a bit. I didn't manage to get through all I needed to. I promised my post-grad I'd look over our absolutely, utterly final draft of a paper today and I hadn't finished.'

'I can take you there. It's on my way.'

'No it's ok thanks. It's not far and you really go in the other direction, do you not? It's not cold anyway. It's quite nice out.'

'Are you around over the vacation?'

'I haven't got any plans to go away at the moment. I don't really see that I'll be able to. My mother's just out of hospital and things like that. What about yourself?'

'Look, the car's just outside. Come on. Jump in. I'll take you there and then you'll be able to leave work all the sooner.'

When we're outside, he opens the passenger door for me then goes round to the driver's seat.

'Put your bag in the back. So – if you're not going away, maybe we could meet up? There are some good concerts on. There's a couple of Requiems.'

He makes them sound like a pair of bookends.

'What about it? Shall I give you a ring?'

'I guess. I'm not sure I would be comfortable going out to a concert or something.'

'Why not? We've known each other a long time. There's no pressure.'

'I know. I'm just not sure.'

'I'll phone you anyway and see what you think about it nearer the time.'

'Here we are. I need to get out here -just drop me, will you? You don't need to park the car. This is fine.'

He pulls over and jumps round to open the door for me, even though I've tried hard to get out quickly.

'Remember. No pressure. It would just be nice to have company. I've bought tickets already so they would be going to waste.'

He watches me as I hurry up to the door. What's the bloody combination for the lock again?

11.

In my childhood there were five tall poplar trees at the end of the garden. On summer days we could tell the time better from them than from the sundial set in the red and black square tiles. The sun tracked across the trees from left to right. Seldom higher than the tips, it would disappear as it crossed the trunk and the spotlight where I sunbathed would go out. As the shadows grew longer the sky would turn from blue to the muted shades of a late day. I would lie on the grass, a thin mat keeping out damp but not the hard bumps below. With the sun dropping, the honeysuckle smell would come out. I could hear my rabbits scuttling in their hutches. God forgive me for so confining them. Yet I loved them desperately. They came further up in my prayers than all my cousins. Then came a day when I decided to breed them. They fought fiercely in a terribly flurry and separating them left me with a permanent moon-shaped scar on my finger. I didn't know anything about mating. When they eventually died, unwittingly poisoned by contaminated sawdust, I tried hard to mourn as much for the one I favoured less. The vet conducted a post-mortem, giving me its tail as a memento. I still have it. Their death has ever since been the standard of my grief. Is this worse? Is this the same?

'Your brother's coming home'.

My mother is bustling.

'You lay the table. And bring in some lettuce from the garden. I'm glad I've got enough cold meat. But maybe he won't want salad. He'll have had enough of that in Spain.'

I guess she thinks that because we eat salad in summer, in

Spain they'll eat it all the time, it being so hot. She's never been to Spain. Never been abroad.

'You go to the butcher's. Here, take my purse. Get six chops. I'll do the potatoes.'

He'd been hitchhiking in Europe after being released from university and had ended up in Spain. Now he's come back – brown, hairy, full of stories. They'd been stopped by the police in four different countries. Was that a record? I, on the other hand, was only allowed contained and supervised trips organised by the school.

The day after he came home my letter of acceptance to university arrived. My mother brought it upstairs where I was still in bed and waited while I opened it. The long summer lay ahead. The time beyond that was legislated for, now, though it remained undefined and inchoate. I had some ideals about learning, not much else. Philosophy sounded good.

"I would be grateful if you would appear...entitled to bring a representative..."

The formal letter from HOD is inviting me to discuss not just my designation, as I was expecting, but my 'future plans'. I can bring as advocate a member of the Union if I so wish.

Susan Johnstone is one of the two union reps. The other is the HOD who, in addition to heading numerous committees in the university, is Chairman of the local School Board. He's even President of the Common Room Committee in the building, overseeing the supply of coffee and plastic cups.

'You've nothing to worry about,' Susan is explaining to me in her office. 'You were given tenure on a specific contract. They can't take that away retrospectively.'

'But what about the job regrading?'

'You can't be worse off.'

'In what terms though? I appreciate they can't pay me less but that's not the point. Anyway, it sounds as if it might be even worse than status or money. It might be my actual job.'

'No chance. No worries.'

She's very calm. Her hands are unmoving on her lap. I wonder what motivates her. Later, I send an email to HOD agreeing to a meeting next week. I name my advocate. It crosses my mind that I might need a real one some time in the future.

'Dr Lamb?'
    'Yes?'
'It's Charlie. Charlie Broadhurst.'
I repeat the name to give me time.
    'Rosie's friend.'
    'Of course. I'm sorry. She told me about you. How is she today?'
I had wondered whether Charlie might be the father of Rosie's baby.
    'She's still in hospital. But she's getting out later today.'
    'Is she ok? I mean… what happened?'
    'She's lost it. They operated on her first thing today. They're saying she can go home later.'
    'What a shame. That's so sad. How is she?'
    'I think she would like you to visit again.'
    'Of course. Do you mean 'home home', as with her mother, or home to her flat?'

It's his place, which turns out to be on the ground floor of a large, flatted building. The name plates are all temporary – paper labels stuck on top of the metal plate, some half torn off. The social stratification of an area can be read from its nameplates, I've always thought, in the same way that social class and size of dog are inversely related.

Inside, though, it's sanded floorboards, white walls and the beige plus taupe tones of grown ups rather than purple and black walls with posters. Charlie, now I see him, is short, curly headed, muscular. He's bursting out of himself. He leaves Rosie and me alone in the bedroom. She's lying flat under the sheets, looking smaller than ever and very wan. When I last saw her she was animatedly talking about time travel. Energy makes people look bigger.

'I'm sorry for dumping this on you,' she says some way into our talk.

She starts to describe the moment she lost the baby. How she'd looked into the dish they'd left to see what it looked like. And how at that point some church people had arrived in the ward to sing hymns. They're singing 'Amazing Grace', she says, while she's staring at what looks like pieces of liver in a small metal dish.

She blows her nose. I don't say anything, just look at her.

'So there,' she goes on. 'I feel a bit better now.'

'It sounds awful.'

'Don't tell anyone, will you not?'

After a while I ask her about Charlie.

'I hope he can cook some?' I say.

'Charlie's ok. He and I go back a long way.'

How long when you're only twenty? It's like students talking about best friends they'd met on holiday three months ago. Was I once like that?

'You know how you asked me about the scanner?' she continues.

'Yes?'

'When I'd been a subject?'

'Yes.'

'You think it's to do with the baby, don't you? Losing the baby?'

'I don't know, Rosie, I really don't know. I can't say that – well, obviously, you know I can't say that. But it did cross my mind.'

'I worked it out – I would have been six or seven weeks pregnant when it was done.'

'What did they say at the hospital? Did they discuss why you might have lost the baby? Did anyone talk to you?'

'The doctor who did the operation. She was nice. Except she kept saying 'No problem.' I don't know why that's so annoying. She meant well. I just ...it just seemed a bit like she was talking about finding my suitcase or something. Now I feel rotten, saying that.'

'What did she say to you?'

'She asked about any illnesses and that sort of thing. I had had a virus – I know that. It was when I was about five weeks pregnant, I worked out. She said it might have been that. But she told me that lots of babies – except she didn't use the word 'babies' – she talked about 'embryos' and 'cells' and stuff. Anyway, lots are lost – die off, without people even knowing they're pregnant.'

'Did you mention the imaging scan?'

'See before I tell you – will you say first whether you think I should have? Please? Then I'll really know what you think.'

'Of course. I do think you should have told her.'

'And I did. Good.'

'What did she say?'

'She looked kind of grim. She said it's just possible that it had been related, that even though it's generally safe, they don't ever use these scans on pregnant women unless there's a good medical reason.'

'I'm glad you told her. Did she ask you who carried out the scan?'

'She repeated the name, actually, when I said it.'

'Really?'

'Do you think it might go any further?'

'It's possible. I don't know what protocols they follow. I wouldn't be totally surprised though.'

'Oh dear. Do you think I'll have to give evidence or anything?'

'It's not going to Court, Rosie.'

'It's just that I don't want Professor Mason to get into trouble.'

'Don't worry about that. He's a grown up. He can look out for himself.'

'Will you let me know if there's anything going on?'

'I would like to think that *you* would be told before me,' I tell her. 'In the eyes of the university it's nothing to do with me, remember'

'I just mean that you might hear gossip or something.'

She starts to cry again. I'm thinking, here I am again. Funny sort of life.

12.

'**M**adeleine!'
Simon is exasperated.
'Don't you agree?'
'Like turkeys agreeing to Christmas?'

I notice my cliché. And it's bad enough feeling like a waste of space at work.

'You took advantage,' he continues. 'I was always there for whenever you could fit me in to your schedule. I wasn't supposed to have any feelings or thoughts on the matter....'

'That's really not fair. I know I called the shots a lot of the time but that was because you were working on your book. You were always available simply because you weren't doing much else. So what was I supposed to do?'

'It was always you phoning me only when you had a gap in your social life.'

'That's not true. I don't know how many times I suggested going out and you said you had to work.'

'I don't remember that at all.'

'Well it happened. It happened lots. Or even, we would be out somewhere and you would get into a bad mood – remember that time in Lambo's when we were having coffee and thinking about going to the pictures and you started getting twitchy and you ended up just leaving. I mean, I was still drinking my bloody coffee and you walked off in a sudden funk about your work.'

'I don't think I would have done that.'

'I'm sure you don't. We never think these things of ourselves. I don't either. But you did.'

'In that case I'm sorry. Don't you see,' he goes on, 'I just needed you to talk me down. The way you did before. You talked me through stuff and it helped and things were ok. I just needed…I guess I wanted a bit of mothering.'

'But I'm not your mother. I never was. That was the problem – I was becoming your mother. And it doesn't work.'

'So you think that's what went wrong?'

'Between us? One of the things, I suppose.'

'But how? How were you my mother?'

'Because I was always the one to make decisions. Even if it was just about what TV programme to watch, you always said it was up to me. Now…'

'Christ. You should be so lucky,' he says.

'I know. I know that's lucky in a way. But if it applies to everything…I just felt I was the strong one and that you depended on me. It scared me a little, to be honest. You said to me once, early on, that you felt safe. I remember, you had your arms around me and you said that you felt safe.'

'So?'

'*I* didn't feel safe. It was fine for you but sometimes I need a bit of looking after too. A bit of succourance too.'

'Why didn't you tell me? We were together for two years and you didn't tell me.'

'Even if I'd realised, I'm not sure I would have told you. It doesn't work that way. You don't just change someone's character by telling them that you want them to be different. What could you have done? Anyway, these things aren't always clear. I mean, you don't articulate them at the time. It was only after…and anyway, I did try to say to you – remember, that night when I suggested we went for a walk and I was saying to you that I didn't think it was working?'

'Excuse me, I was saying to you that I didn't think it was working.'

'What?'

'I wasn't happy with the way things were going. I was the one who suggested that there needed to be some changes if we were going to go on.'

'Are you trying to tell me that you broke it off with me?'

'I started it. I was the one who introduced the topic.'

'You were not. I remember we were walking in complete silence and I was saying to myself, when we get to the lamppost at the corner I'll say it. Then, when we get to the postbox I'll say it. You weren't talking at all. You were in one of your huffs.'

'Huffs! What do you mean huffs?' he says.

'What huffs always mean. When someone stops talking to someone else. And not because they've finished speaking.'

'I don't go into huffs.'

'You fucking well do. You did it all the time.'

'I have never been in the huff with you.'

'You once didn't speak to me for three weeks.'

'What!'

'Three weeks. Three. Weeks. It was before you went off to Australia for that conference.'

'That was after we broke up.'

'That is not the point. The bloody point is that you did not speak to me for weeks and it was me that broke the silence. It was me that sent a note saying I'd heard you were going to Australia and that we should get together some time before then.'

'You're mad.'

'I'm not fucking mad. Listen, I was always the one to bring us back together after your little freak-outs. I don't know how you can be so obtuse. So fucking lacking in self-awareness.'

'You're the psychologist.'

'Fat lot of good it does with you.'

'Don't be so rude. You think you're nice. I bet you see yourself as 'nice'. Other people think you're nice but they don't know you.'

'I am nice.'

'Pray tell me how.'

'I'm happy for other people's happiness. I go on smiling after I've smiled at people I'm passing. That's nice. That's two ways I'm nice. How do you want me to be nice?'

'I want you to be nice to me. And I wish you wouldn't swear the way you do.'

'What's it to you Simon? Just what is it to you? We are no longer an item. We broke up three years ago. You have been with someone else since then. I've been out with other people. Christ, you're still with someone at this moment.'

'Did you not feel we were special then?'

'What about Rosalyn? Is she not special?'

'I thought she was. I'm not sure.'

'It's not the point anyway. The point is, I did think we were special for a while but then I stopped feeling that and I broke it off. The way I remember it anyway. But I suppose it doesn't matter now.'

'It does don't you see? We were so good together. It seems terrible to throw it away.'

'Simon, why are you coming to me now, saying this?'

'I've always thought that . . .ever since we broke up.. .'

'But you've been going out with Rosalyn for nearly a year.'

'I suppose that's why I've realised how good we were. I keep comparing her with you.'

'That's not very nice.'

'How come? I can't help my feelings. You were the first person I really loved. I didn't realise that you were, well, unique. I was fed up with things, like the way you downgraded me, and then when you were being nasty to me towards the end – you were really quite dismissive, you know. You can be quite harsh when you talk to people sometimes.'

'I'm talking about Rosalyn. You're being very disloyal to her, coming to me with all this.'

'What am I supposed to do? Break it off and come back and formally ask you to get together again?'

'I suppose that would be the most noble way of doing it. But there's no point. A: it's unrealistic and B: I can't go back. We had good reasons for breaking up and I don't see that they would have just disappeared. I've gone back to someone before and it doesn't work. The same problems just come up again. The point is, I'm happy just being friends.'

'How can you be? We had such a good sex life. That doesn't disappear. Do you not remember that holiday?'

'Please. Stop it. It's over. Good sex lives do disappear. They disappear when people go off each other.'

'I never went off you. I just wanted things to change.'

'That's what I meant when I said I had broken it off. I didn't just want some things to *change*. I wanted out.'

'Don't tell me you can't still feel something between us? Some sort of pull?'

'I feel warmly towards you Simon. I do. At least, I did before tonight. I really wasn't expecting this. You're still going out with Rosalyn.'

'If I weren't with her…would that make a difference?'

'No, I really don't think so. I came to feel differently about you, Simon. Not the way a girlfriend should. Just the way a friend should. They're quite different.'

'I've never stopped fancying you. You don't know how it drives me crazy just to see you cross your ankles. You don't know the effect you have on me.'

'You've no right to do this. Quite apart from the fact that you're still with Rosalyn, I've never given you any encouragement, have I? Never given you reason to think that there was hope?'

'When I came back from Australia you were so welcoming. I remember you gave me such a hug. I began to think that you felt something.'

'To which you responded by starting up a relationship with Rosalyn?'

'Were you jealous then?'

'I saw our friendship threatened. And it was. I was right. We don't see much of each other at all these days. But it was still quite different from wanting to go back to you. I didn't then and I don't now. I'm sorry, Simon, I really don't. It wouldn't work.'

I would have my life full of loose ends. No friends ever lost. Old lovers still possibilities. But feelings can turn on a thought and sometimes you can never get rid of that thought.

13.

'**S**he's what?'

Tony's come in.

'I just heard it from Richard,' he says.

'When did it happen?'

'At the weekend I gather.'

My Advocate, the union rep. Susan Johnstone, appears to have gone AWOL. Some sort of breakdown.

'Great. Bloody great. God I'm selfish. Poor woman. No. I do feel for her. But she seemed so composed.'

'She's had a rotten case on the go. Management have been screwing over someone in Eng. Lit. I believe.'

'That's her job though. I would have thought that kind of thing was routine. There must be more to it surely?'

Tony shrugs.

'Isn't there always? But then I've no idea.'

'It could be nothing to do with work, of course,' he goes on. 'Maybe one of her kids is ill.'

I'm thinking how little I like people using the word 'kids' instead of 'children'. It's sort of disrespectful in a way I can't explain.

'I'll keep you posted,' he says and hands over a pile of marking.

'When's this due back?' I ask.

'Thursday.'

'What? Chrissake, that's only three days away. How many are there?'

'Two hundred and ten. That's seventy a day. See, I worked it out for you.'

'Very funny. Tony that's just not possible. I couldn't do it even if I marked non-stop and didn't eat or go to the loo or... nothing.'

'Ok ok. Just do your best. I know it's more than Chateau Despair dictates.'

Chateau Despair, where Suits manage the provision of educational products for our clients.

'By the way,' he says, 'the case of Owen versus the State continues.'

'What are you talking about?'

'The chap who appealed in the summer.'

'Against his lower second?'

'The very one. I've just been to the Faculty Appeals Committee and they've upheld it. It's been remitted to the Board for reconsideration.'

'How can they? Just how far are our masters prepared to go? They let in anyone who can spell their name and then we get blamed if the student fails to get the degree they want. What were the grounds again for this guy? Was it something to do with extra time?'

'He was Disability - got an extra ten minutes every hour. This year he applied to get fifteen. The trouble is, he wasn't told the outcome until the day before his first exam.'

'So?'

'It stressed him, apparently, not knowing in advance how much extra time he was going to get – ten or fifteen minutes.'

'Dear god. So how did he verify it, this burden of stress?'

'He got a consultant psychologist to carry out psychometric tests. This guy produced a measure of state anxiety.'

'How do you measure 'state anxiety' retrospectively? It's supposed to show what you feel on the day.'

'I brought this up, believe me. The defence was that "his client was instructed to imagine himself back in time" to just before the exam.'

'And the committee accepted that?'

'They thought it suggestive enough, at least, to refer the whole thing back for further consideration.'

'So – another Exam Board. And if we refuse to budge?'

'Presumably he'll try to take it further. He seemed pretty sure of himself. Personally I'd be mortified knowing that all the staff thought I was a lower second. The fact is, though, he could take it outside the university if it doesn't succeed here.'

'I wonder how much all this is costing the university. If you budget the time for one Dean, several professors, lots of senior lecturers...'

'Thousands. Tens of thousands of pounds? And if it gets remitted to this outside body, then tens and tens of thousands.'

'He could have bought a degree somewhere for that.'

'It's not his money. By the way, are you remembering the Christmas bash tomorrow? Are you going?'

I'm remembering when I was a student and had flu when I sat an exam. It didn't occur to me to tell anybody.

Rosie sounds cheerful on the phone.

'I'm going home for Christmas so at least I'll get fed.'

'Why, what did you have for dinner tonight?'

'Toast, custard and black coffee.'

'That's terrible. Are you broke?'

'Yeah. I've not been able to do my job you see. And Charlie's run out too.'

'I could give you money. Think of it as a Christmas present.'

'No. Thanks though, but I'm going home tonight. It'll be ok. When term starts again I'll be fit to go back to my job. Have you heard anything about Professor Mason?'

'Nothing. But I'll be having a meeting with him soon about other things and I'll bring it up. I'm sure the university will be on to it. How are you getting home, by the way? Do you need a lift? Would you like a lift, I mean. I've got the Department party but I could take you before that if you like?'

But Charlie is borrowing his brother's car. Thank god I'm

past going home. Thank god I'm protected by my mother's unhinged thoughts:

'We're allowed to intervene,' she said to me the other day.

'In what?'

'Everything,' she said.

Sounds like a good motto.

Christmas time is so hard. So hard going out every night, drinking every night, putting on your public face. But it's old chums tonight – all women though not a women's group. I'm put out that Lizzie's appeared though it's apparently only for ten minutes or so. She often doesn't come at all and will renege if there's anything better on offer – something where men are involved, in short. We should have elbowed her out ages ago but we were too nice. I thought her charming at first because she makes you feel that you matter. But it's calculated flattery. Part of it means sharing confidences. It was a while before I realised that her secrets actually belonged to other people. She would tell you about a friend's abortion, not her own.

'Dilly,' she's saying to one of the group as I go in. 'When's your cousin coming?'

And how long was he staying for? Was he staying with her? What was it he does again – did she say he was an academic? How old was he? Louisa, who's hosting the evening, butts in robustly.

'I must tell you about my date last week.'

'Yes,' we practically shout. We haven't forgotten. Just saving the best till last.

'He's lovely.'

'What's he like? What does he look like?'

'Not too tall. But tall enough for me.'

Louisa is petite.

'I told you he was an art teacher, didn't I? He's still enthusiastic, though– he's only been there since the summer. Mind you, I suppose you can see the signs already. He refers to his boss as "the little shit". Or wait a minute - was it "the little bastard"? We went to an opening, anyway, in the Bilcliffe Gallery. It was good. I actually liked some of the paintings which made it ok to drink their wine. I nearly bought one of the paintings, in fact. They reminded me of the Group of Seven. The Canadian lot, you know?'

We're making our way through a mound of blinis with cream cheese and smoked salmon; knocking back pink cava. Oh the high life.

After Lizzie leaves, Marcia, who copes so well in spite of her husband, starts talking about a woman she suspects is after her husband. A mutual friend of theirs and someone known to all of us. She's suspicious because she found a used condom after being away. We don't ask whether she deliberately went through the bin. Her marriage was only ever sixty percent.

'She's so bloody boastful too,' she's saying about her suspected rival. 'She was talking last time about how she and her husband have decided that they're not going to be highflyers. They're going to devote themselves to their "creative gifts".'

'Covering up inadequacies, in other words,' says Dill.

'In my view, she does it very well,' I say. 'I wish I could cover up mine so competently.'

'She's always lucky, by her own account, isn't she?' says Louisa. 'She could fall in the river and bring out a salmon.'

'No,' says Dill. 'She would bring out a sardine and declare it a salmon.'

14.

'**P**rofessor Lamb?'

I decide to let the professor bit pass. The voice on the phone is middle-aged. A grown up.

'Hello Professor Lamb. I was just looking for a bit of advice.'

'Yes?'

'My daughter has to return her form tonight and we thought it might be useful to get some further information from you.'

'Yes?'

I'm thinking the student must be ill, that she has to get her mother to phone.

'She wants to be a child psychologist and we were just wondering whether she should be doing more science options than language ones because she's quite keen on languages, but someone's told us that she needs maths and statistics.'

I'm not following this very well.

'What year is she in just now?'

'Second.'

'It'll be determined by what Faculty she's in. She needs to do the Statistics 1B, of course, before going on to honours.'

'I don't think we know anything about that.'

'The statistics option?'

'No. They don't teach that.'

'Excuse me...by the way what's your name please? I should have asked, sorry.'

'Mrs Dempster.'

'And what's your daughter's name?'

'Susan.'

'And she's in second year?'

'Yes.'

'Her Advisor of Studies must have told her that she has to do the Statistics option in her first or second year. It's a prerequisite for getting into honours. She really should have been told this. It's in the handbook too.'

'She didn't get a handbook.'

'Has she actually enrolled in the class? I mean, she's not just been turning up at lectures all term has she, without being registered?'

'They just move from one year into the next.'

'I'm sorry, Mrs Dempster, I just don't understand what's been happening with your daughter – with Susan. May I ask why you're dealing with it rather than her? It's quite unusual.'

'She's only thirteen.'

'Pardon?'

'She's still at school.'

'So…I don't understand. What was that about making choices, then, to be a child psychologist?'

'She's got to fill in her form for tomorrow, saying what her choices are for third year so that…'

'Third year at school?'

'That's right.'

'And why are you asking me this?'

'She wants to be a child psychologist. I told you. She needs to know what to start specialising in.'

'Mrs Dempster, how did you get my number? Did one of the secretaries put you through?'

'I saw it on the web.'

'Well, first of all there's actually no such thing as a "child psychologist" and…'

'Oh but there is. I know someone who's one.'

'You may know a psychologist who works with children but that's a different thing. You don't train to be 'a child psychologist'. You train as an educational psychologist, or a clinical one, and then go on to work with children.'

'So what should she choose? What am I going to put on this form?'

I give her the lecture about young people choosing the things that interest them most since that's the best route to success. We already have enough students who're shipwrecked on their parents' choices.

'Thank you very much Professor Lamb,' she says finally, cutting through my homily. 'You've been most helpful.'

I put down the receiver and give it a two fingered salute.

Fucking poncy fucking mothers.

The Department is unrecognisable on the evening of the Party. The tables in the large Conference Room are reorganised and decked out. Staff and postgrads are hastily taking their seats so that they don't have to sit with enemies. I spot Mason holding court with senior staff at the top table.

The food has been laid out on tables in the corridor outside with little flags explaining the dishes that people have brought: 'Vegetarian lasagne'; 'Couscous with roasted vegetables'; 'Boeuf Bourguignon'. There's a big dish of mashed turnip in a plain glass bowl. Malcolm, its owner, explains his particular way of making it, which involves putting a whole turnip in the microwave for fifteen minutes. There is something very impressive about both the technique and his enthusiasm. His contribution has required rather less effort than my tiramisu, which had, after a couple of hours, required the creation of a lattice of cardboard strips across the bowl over which I sprinkled cocoa powder, leaving an almost professional finish.

I'm not saying this turnip man is an enemy. He might be if there were degrees of enemy but I don't think there are in quite the same way that there are degrees of friend and degrees of marriage. Enemy is a kind of all or nothing thing. He sits opposite me when we return with our full plates. He's wearing his favourite corduroy suit. His hair is combed over from back to front in the way of Strategy number two. Number one is combing it all across the head from one side to the other, which is more popular. His beard still has flecks of breakfast on it. He starts telling me about his sinus trouble but how he's worked out how to clear them by standing on his head in the bath in the morning, holding his nose and blowing. I put down my fork.

'Are you coming for dessert?' he asks.

'I might give it a miss,' I say. 'You go ahead'.

Very soon everyone is chemically altered. The cocktails have been worthy of litigation and are doubly lethal for hitting empty stomachs. The party hats are on, Mason is looking over his speech and the first person to fall over has already done so. And I have had an impressive chat up:

'You're looking fucking gorgeous tonight Madeleine.'

Wow.

'I just wish I were... ten years older,' he goes on.

I must put this in my diary. Someone behind bumps into him, knocking his arm against my breast. I just give him a smile and move on.

When the karaoke starts, I leave, glad not to have crossed Mason's path. I need to walk home. Not drunk but drunk enough not to care too much. I suppose that's why drink is so popular.

Next morning the photographs from the party are up on the web. Our eyes are all red and no-one looks as good as they felt at the time. There are emails too. The secretary complaining on behalf of the cleaner about someone being sick on the front steps. Two of the postgrads saying, 'I'm not a tight arse but I'd just like to say shame on whomever came into Roger and I's office tonight and help themselves to lager.' It finishes: 'I hope your happy with yourselves. At a time of year when we're supposed to be nice to one another, I hope something spikey hits whomever it was right up the bum.'

When I get home I draft a letter to the university's Health and Safety Committee. 'It has come to my attention that Professor Mason of the Psychology Department recently conducted an MRI scan on a student without observing the guidelines set out by the Faculty Ethics Committee. I consider this to be a very serious matter. I am willing to attend a meeting to discuss the details but would ask in the meantime that this be kept confidential. I would particularly request that my name is not associated with the complaint since it would compromise my position in the Department which is delicate at this point in time for a number of reasons.'

That's the heart of it anyway.

15.

'**Y**ou fucking bitch!'

When someone comes knocking at my door a few days after the party I think it's a chum with a Christmas card or some invitation. At worst it might be a student but they're supposed to have decamped for the vacation. I don't expect Mason. His face is too red for someone with his dodgy heart.

'You fucking bitch,' he says again.

'Don't you dare speak to me like that.'

My heart is immediately thumping hard and I'm glad the desk is shielding me.

'And don't you dare go behind my back and report me,' he goes on.

'What are you talking about?'

'"Professor Mason...", "MRI scan...", "contrary to guidelines...".'

He starts quoting phrases from my letter to Human Resources.

'Excuse me,' I interrupt. 'Where did you get this from?'

'That's none of your fucking business.'

'Will you kindly leave my office now. I am not going to take abuse from you or anyone else. I'm going to report you to HR right now.'

I reach for the phone.

'We'll see about that. Don't you forget there's just you and me here and whose word do you think they'll take?'

'I should think they already know your reputation for rudeness and intransigence Professor Mason.'

'How dare you, you little cow. And do you think they would care anyway? Do you think that they're going to set more store by your discontent than mine? Just how much grant money have you brought in? What are your esteem indicators? Do you get invited to give keynote addresses all over the world? Oh yes and when was it you last had something published?'

'None of that sanctions your speaking to me like that.'

'Like I said young lady. You can bleat all you like but there's no-one here to notice. Who will be on your side? Just tell me that, you nasty little cunt of a woman.'

'Have you ever considered that you might have Tourette's?'

He turns and on his way out kicks the end filing cabinet so hard that a plant falls over spilling earth on the carpet.

I can't move. I try to tell myself that in the end he's just a little guy with halitosis. But it doesn't work. I make myself breathe slowly to cool my heart down. Then I can make a plan.

When I do phone Human Resources I can't get hold of the appropriate person. The one I sent the letter to is "Out of office at present". At the loo? On holiday? Deceased perhaps.

I have two lines of complaint. The breach of confidence that they've perpetrated, and Mason's harassment. It's two hours before I track this person down, during which time I've been in Tony's office getting solace as well as establishing a record of what's happened. It will make it more believable in court. I need to get in touch with the Union too and I wonder briefly whether Susan is making any progress with her problems. I'd forgotten about her again. People disappear all the time and you don't notice they've gone. I guess I'm just a stick figure in other people's landscapes too.

A Santa Claus brooch is holding my mother's cardigan together. The material is bobbled now but at least it's not a fleece. There's no excuse for fleeces, especially beige ones. It's just as well I've brought her a new cardigan for Christmas. Apart from sweets it's the only suitable present left. Last year Miles and I gave identical navy ones with gold buttons. Both have since gone missing though they haven't yet appeared on other residents, unlike her glasses. At least she's managed to keep her own dentures. They fit well, sitting nicely on the stumps of her lower jaw. The few teeth of her own that she has left are very brown. I wonder if they still bother to brush them for her.

She's been asleep and when I waken her she smiles but it's her social smile and not one of recognition. I've brought some old photographs. She doesn't know her brothers and sisters but she does say "That's my father. And that's my mother" so I know she's still in there somewhere.

She strokes my face now and says "Oh it's you Maddie. Dear, dear Maddie" and for an instant I think she's always loved me after all. I'm overwhelmed with regret, such regret. But the moment passes. She's soft because she's lost her power. She's just another old lady and I've been brought up to be kind.

Her neighbour is now picking his nose and examining the findings. He stops to comment on our photos.

'You were a looker,' he says to my mother. 'So's your daughter,' he goes on, leaning over and peering at me. He's wearing a paper hat from the Christmas lunch and I can see the big hairs in his nostrils. 'Yes, you're not a bad bit of stuff.'

At the next table an old boy is telling a new boy how it is:

'This *is* the promised land. You just need to get used to it, you know.'

The new boy has a fit of coughing and some of his biscuit lands on the floor. I go to pick it up even though it's not my responsibility but when I look down I see it's his teeth.

My first sense of betrayal was at Christmastime. I must have been about eight. Santa wrote back using the coloured pencil from the kitchen drawer. What else, I wondered. But everything was for our own good, even deception. When she lied to the neighbours about why I'd left home at thirteen it was for my own protection she said. The incident – oh but it was longer than an incident – was never referred to again. A lacuna in my past.

Anything that didn't fit the script was left out. We never had any inappropriate emotions and roses bloomed in December. I think we weren't meant to have any emotions at all. When my father died, she talked brightly about trivia in the funeral car.

'Don't you start,' she said at my tears. 'You'll set me off.'

When am I supposed to cry? Will I cry when she goes?

'Goodbye mother,' I say now.

I kiss her on the cheek, avoiding the rough mole. We don't kiss in my family but somehow now it's expected. I must try harder to enjoy my life.

At my brother's house for the Christmas meal, I try to preserve each good moment in my head. There are no parents squashing us this year. I don't have to swear to annoy them. So I say to myself, this is nice. I am enjoying this. I am happy.

Even though my mother has always preferred my brother, I still love him and his wife and their child. She, my little niece sitting in the highchair next to me, spoons some cranberry sauce into her mouth then spits it out.

'That's horrible,' she says and we all laugh. But then I start I imagining myself at a disciplinary meeting where Mason rehearses his calumny against me, humiliating me. That's horrible, I'll say, and spit as violently as I can.

Christmas day and I'm thinking about Mason.

Two days later I'm back in the Department, if only to reduce the eventual pile of email that would await me otherwise. It's almost not worthwhile taking time off. There are the usual emails from people I've sent a card to who didn't send one back, talking about how they don't set much store by Christmas but would like to say Happy New Year. Other offerings - outings, the cinema. I'd thought I'd find one from Rosie but don't, so email her, feeling guilty. In my head, though, I've had her tucked away safely at home with a benign mother. When all that is done, I turn to the hard mail. Mostly circulars from publishers but one from Human Resources that was hidden in the bundle from my pigeonhole. Christ what now? I thought that everything was arranged – there would be a meeting to 'discuss my future'. This is worse. A disciplinary meeting, they're calling it now. Rather pre-emptive, I think. A sense of smallness comes over me and I want a mother to take care of me.

The whole place is quiet. It seems as if there's no-one else in – I tap on Tony's door without much hope- but I do hear noises when I pass Mason's room. Usually I avoid this route but today I don't expect him to be there. There's a moaning sound from inside. What? I can't make out whether it's Mason himself, or a woman's voice or even his computer. I can't just walk on. I move my head closer to the door. It is Mason, I can tell. But he sounds in distress. His voice breaks into clicks then another moan, more like one of anguish than before.

He has a bad heart, I say to myself. I hate him but I can't leave him dying if it comes to the bit. I tap the door. There's no response and the noises continue, only louder. Dear god I'll need to do something.

'Professor Mason?'

I say his name again, banging the door. An anguished cry. Fuck it. I push the door open.

He's sitting in his swivel chair facing me, turned away from the desk. His computer is on in the background. On the screen a young blonde woman is dipping up and down on top of a man lying naked, one hand palpating her breast, his other arm stretched out on the floor. The woman's face is upturned and inert, as if she doesn't know the man. The camera zooms into the zone of his penis disappearing into her, reappearing, as they engage. They look like a mechanical toy. But before that...before that I have seen Mason. Mason with staccato noises coming from his lips, his face twisting, white stuff at the sides of his mouth; his body jerking, the chair rocking. Not sexual ecstasy but an epileptic fit. Mason so out of control that he can't pull up his trousers to cover his swollen purple penis.

Only his eyes are still as he looks at me.

16.

At New Year I manage two parties. My chums, most of whom I like, have got together at the first one. At twelve when the bells bring in the New Year, I have no-one's eyes to look at. In thirty seconds I'm kissing five people but the loneliness has done its harm. Marcia's husband is invading my space. You can never point this out: personal space is not measurable but felt. The other person would just act hurt and you'd be left with the sense of shame. It's easier to go to party number two, though it's already halfway through the night.

'Happy New Year!'.

In the street, a voice comes out of the dark. A large man holds out his hand. God forbid he tries to kiss me, even if it is New Year. Instead he takes my hand in his and raises it to his lips. He's not drunk and I recognise him from the university.

'You're Psychology, aren't you?'

'Yes. Madeleine.'

'I remember seeing you at a joint Exam Board. I thought you were Drama and lost the bet. That's how I know you're Psychology. You've got to pass the time somehow,' he adds.

'Sorry, I don't remember you. I kind of know your face though. You're…?'

'French. Philip.'

'Ah. Nice. The Department, I mean.'

'I'm not so sure. I guess we all feel the same about our departments. Where are you off to?'

'Another party.'

'On your own?'

'In between times,' I say.

What an idiot. He means now. At this moment. He's not asking about your love life.

'Ok if I walk with you?'

'Is it not out of your way?'

'It doesn't matter. I'm going to a party too, but I'm not expected at a particular time. As you might guess, from it being in the middle of the night.'

It turns out he's off to the party I've just left.

'I'll walk with you wherever, if that's ok?'

His formality reminds me of my father. It's a sign of weakness that the offer seems attractive. That lonely feeling at midnight is still working its way out.

At the second party I find Mel half asleep on the couch with Lola, both very drunk and both in pyjamas. Drinking gin, the drink of the disappointed. Philip has dropped me off and there are only a few women left at this one.

'It's Amy!' shouts Lola.

When she's drunk she says I look like Amy Winehouse. I'm the opposite if such things are possible. Why are we supposed to laugh at insults? Is it being a good sport? I look around for a drink. The gin is apparently finished.

'Why do you wear all that make-up?' she persists.

'You tell me why not.'

'I think it's the least one can do. I mean, what's it all about? You're turning yourself into a little object for men. The objectification of women. You should know all about that.'

'Lola I've seen you fussing for ages with your hair. I've seen you put powder on your face. What's the difference?'

'I don't do all the eyes stuff. You know that courtesans used to put deadly nightshade in their eyes? Made their pupils bigger so that they looked interested in those boring fucks of men? Bella Donna, you know?'

'I do know. I think I was the one who told you, in fact. Anyway, lay off will you? I don't see any difference between me wearing eye make-up and you putting on powder. And I don't need this.'

She seems to smirk but maybe it's the drink.

'What's wrong with you? Why are you feeling sorry for yourself?' she says.

At least, I think that's what she says. Her speech isn't that clear.

'Oh shut up Lola!'

Mel says this in too good a natured way. Yes shut the fuck up, I say under my breath. I don't think I'll stay long.

There are dregs of drink in the kitchen. A little white wine, warmed up now. Signs of desperation – the holiday liqueur bottles have been brought out and people have been drinking Limoncello and Calisaya. Possibly even together. I take the remainder of the white and it's as awful as I envisaged. Mel appears waving her empty glass. Her mascara has smudged and her left eyelid droops the way it always does when she's tired or drunk. We go back a long way. Which doesn't mean to say I approve of everything about her and I daresay she doesn't with me either.

Lola's remarks are only annoying because they resonate with past disapproval. Like the way that people who have died live on inside you, talking back to you in your head.

'What are you thinking of?' asks Mel, putting her arms round me to give me a hug.

'Just rubbish. You know. The past.'

'Christ how old are you? Well, it's New Year. I suppose that's what it's for. Hey – who was that man?'

'Which?'

'The dish, dummy. The one outside. Come on, don't play games with me.'

'Just a guy I met in the street. Well...not quite like that. I sort of know him. He's in the university.'

'Oooh.'

'Don't get excited now. I'm not. He's nice enough I suppose.'

'Are you going to see him again?'

'Why would I? I've just walked along the road with him, that's all.'

'But he's lovely.'

'Mel, he could be a serial killer for all I know.'

'You're always thinking the worst. Of course he's not. He works in the university.'

'That would *make* you a serial killer if you weren't in the first place.'

She laughs.

'No seriously,' I go on, 'If people could get away with murder they would kill all the time.'

'We need to do something about you. I don't know. So young, so cynical.'

'But it's true. They would. I would.'

'You need a man.'

'You'll be telling me next that all I need is a good fuck.'

'That too.'

'Oh do me a favour, will you? And here's another favour. Find me a decent drink, go on.'

The next day at half past twelve my mobile wakens me up. It's Rosie, but a drunk-sounding Rosie.

'You little monkey,' I say. 'Are you still drunk from last night? Happy New Year to you anyway. How are things going? I did email you.'

'I've just found your number.'

'I thought you had it – my mobile? Of course, you're on my mobile now. Sorry. I've just woken up myself.'

'I've been up for hours.'

'Good for you. You must be feeling better then. Sorry – I thought you sounded as if you'd just woken up too.'

'I'm waiting for the rounds but I don't think they're going to happen today. It's a holiday isn't it?'

'It's the first of January. That's always a holiday.'

'Are you on holiday too?'

'Sure. But you know that. I saw you before Christmas and

we talked about what we would be doing in the vacation.'

'I remember now. You weren't going away. That's how I knew to phone.'

'Is there something wrong Rosie? You don't sound quite like yourself.'

'They just keep you waiting. I mean, all the time. Everything. You wait for your meals, you wait for the doctor, wait for...'

'What do you mean? Where are you? Are you not at home?'

'No. I don't think so. No of course I'm not. I'm waiting for them to come and let me out.'

'Where are you waiting? Where are you?'

'With a lot of people. I can't get away from them. There are just too many people around.'

'Where though? Whereabouts?'

'In hospital.'

'I didn't know. Are you back in hospital?'

'Yes. No. Not the same one.'

'Where are you then? Which one? I'm sorry I didn't know you were ill again. Were there complications or what?'

'How do you mean?'

'After your operation? Did you get an infection or something"

'What from?'

'The miscarriage.'

'What miscarriage? I didn't have a miscarriage. They took my baby away.'

'Took it away? You mean, after you lost it?'

'I didn't lose it. They took it out of me.'

'But...just a minute. Are you there on your own? In the hospital? Is there maybe someone I can talk to?'

I hear her calling but can't make out the name.

'She'll talk to you.'

'Who's that then? Who'll talk to me?'

'The nurse.'

'What hospital is it? I'm sorry – asking all these questions. I'm really sorry.'

She gives me the name of the mental hospital and suddenly I want to cry. It's all too sad.

'Hello. This is Sister Baird. Who am I speaking to?'

'Madeleine, Madeleine Lamb. I'm a friend of Rosie's. At least, I'm her tutor at university but I'm also sort of a friend. I mean...'

'Madeleine, you realise that I can't say anything to you. We're very strict about patient confidentiality.'

'I'm very sorry. I was just trying to understand what's going on. The last time I saw Rosie was when she was in hospital...the other hospital. I guess I shouldn't be saying that either.'

'It's all right - we know about that.'

'At that point, that was before Christmas, she was going back home to stay with her mother, to recuperate, to...'

I don't know how to go on.

'It's really best if Rosie tells you herself.'

'Yes, yes of course. Can you put her back on please?'

'I'm really sorry about that Rosie,' I say when she comes back to the phone. 'The nurse has just been telling me – quite right too - that I shouldn't be asking her any questions about you. When did you go into the hospital?'

'About two weeks ago? I don't know.'

'Can I ask why? What's wrong? You don't need to tell me of course.'

I always seem to be saying this to her. I can't find the right bit between concern and intrusion.

'I don't know. Nothing. I thought I was getting out today.'

I hear the sister in the background say 'No, not today.'

'I'll come in to visit. Would that be all right?'

'You can phone my mother too,' she says. 'You can ask her stuff.'

Her little voice sounds very far away. I phone her mother straightaway. She explains that a day or so after Rosie came home from hospital the previous time she became "a bit funny". Her talking was fractured – "broken", was how the mother put it, and her ideas didn't run together as they should. I listen to a kind woman trying to put a decent gloss on her daughter's breakdown. Thank god she's on Rosie's side at any rate. It was the father who insisted on the doctor being phoned and the doctor who'd had her admitted to hospital. Not that her mother disagreed because they couldn't cope.

'What was it that didn't make sense?' I ask her.

'It was all about the baby. She said they'd stolen her baby. That it hadn't been dead but some people had drugged her and cut it out of her.'

'Dear god.'

I know this doesn't help.

'It breaks my heart,' she goes on. 'It just breaks my heart. Then there was the stuff about her professor.'

'Her professor?'

'I don't remember his name. But she said that it was her professor in the university who was the father.'

'The father of her baby?'

She must think I'm obtuse, just repeating everything she says. My mind is jumping about though.

'Do you know the name of her professor?' she asks. 'I know it wasn't true, what she said, but do you know his name anyway? In case we need to warn him or anything.'

'There are several in the department. Professor Love...'

Ironic to think of him first.

'Then there's Mason, and...'

'Mason. I think it was Mason. She said that he was the father of the baby and we were to tell him that their baby had been killed by these people. Of course I didn't do anything about it. The night her father got the doctor in, she was up in her room talking away to this professor like he was there. She sounded very angry too. I don't understand that. You would think that if he were the father she would be feeling...'

She starts to cry.

'I don't know what to think,' she picks up. 'I don't know what's happening. Charlie told us they used the expression "post- partum".'

'Post-partum?'

'It was "post-partum" something else.'

'Was it "depression"? No, you would have remembered that. That's the most common thing though.'

'It was something like "psychiatrist" but not quite.'

'" Psychosis", was it?'

'I think that's it. Do you know anything about it? Can you talk to her? Maybe you could make her see it's all nonsense, what she's saying.'

'I doubt if I could do that, but certainly I'll go and see her. Can I ask, do you know what sort of help she's getting?'

Is she being labelled? Is she embarking on a career as a mental patient? I hear my voice in lectures.

'She's got pills but I don't know what they are. They've slowed her down though. She's awfully tired all the time. She's not like herself at all, even apart from the odd ideas.'

'I wish I'd known sooner.'

'They were talking about shock treatment too.'

So, they're going to fry away Rosie's problems. Happy New Year.

17.

At my 'disciplinary' meeting there are five people present: myself, Susan as Union rep., Mason, plus the Dean of the Faculty – a shiny man - and a woman from Human Resources who is speaking right now.

'I can only apologise, Madeleine, but we seem to have lost some material from your file.'

'What's that?'

'You've indicated that you wrote to HR complaining about an aspect of Professor Mason's behaviour but we can't seem to find any record of it.'

'Not only did I write you, but I also asked you to keep the matter confidential. It subsequently became apparent that you'd discussed the content of my letter with Professor Mason.'

'I don't have any of this in your file.'

'I phoned you to complain about this breach of confidence.'

She frowns, looks down at her papers then looks back at me.

'No. I don't see any of this. Who did you speak to?'

'I believe it was yourself. You are Karen? Right?'

Touche. I had noted the respect she'd given "Professor Mason" and how I was plain "Madeleine".

'I think you must be mistaken. I have no recollection of any such conversation.'

'Dr. Lamb told me about it after it occurred, if that helps,' says Susan. 'I took detailed notes.'

'After what occurred Susan? Do you mean the behaviour that she was complaining about or the phone call she made?'

'Both. Which would you like to hear about?'

'I'm afraid, Susan, that your notes don't constitute primary evidence. You understand, we need to have first hand accounts of what went on. Just like in court – they don't admit hearsay evidence.'

I have an image of battering this smug young woman till the blood runs down her crisp white blouse.

'We're not in court though,' intercedes the Dean. 'We don't need to be so formal. I would like to think that we could resolve things amicably. I'm not in favour of unnecessary conflict.'

He gives a little laugh.

'Dean, I didn't start all this,' I say. 'I came here to defend myself. I have been under attack by Professor Mason for some time now and we need to do something about it. He has consistently undermined my role in the Department, he has cast aspersions on my ability to carry out the job, he has repeatedly assigned more teaching to me than to any other member of staff, he has disparaged my subject area and suggested that my research is not worthwhile. And if that weren't enough, he has bullied me in a very personal way.'

'Hang on, hang on.'

Karen buts in.

'Madeleine, you can't make these accusations without providing evidence to support them. You must understand that we can't just take everybody's word for things? We need to hear all sides of the story.'

'So when Professor Mason denies all this, you'll believe him?'

'Not at all. But he doesn't have to refute a case that hasn't been proven.'

'So he's innocent until proved guilty?'

'Of course.'

'But I'm not?'

'Before we go any further,' she says, 'I need to remind us all that your complaint is not actually on the agenda for today and I do think it's necessary that we keep on track. This meeting, as you know, was called because Professor Mason, in fact, was unhappy with your performance in the job, Madeleine. We have a statutory requirement, in such instances, to issue verbal warnings to people who are seen to be failing. And of course,' she said quickly 'to offer support in furtherance of optimising their attempts to overcome their difficulties and to fully deal with the demands of the job.'

What? Furtherance of what? And has she never heard of split infinitives?

'Is he not required to provide proof?'

'What's that?'

'Does he...'

'Does Professor Mason?'

'Does Professor Mason not need to provide some evidence for his view that I am not performing optimally?'

'He has done.'

'And where is this evidence?' Susan asks.

'It's in Madeleine's file.'

'I'm sure it is,' Susan persists. 'I was asking about the content of the evidence.'

'I can't show you that. Of course, if you wish to apply to see it under the Freedom of Information Act you are at liberty to do so.'

'I will. But in the meantime can you summarise it? We need to know exactly what the complaint is.'

'That's perfectly understandable.'

The Dean looks at the HR woman as he says this.

'Professor Mason,' says the smug young woman, turning to him, 'Can you please just give us a brief outline of your complaint concerning Madeleine's work?'

'I think we would rather have this in writing,' Susan suggests.

Not a good move, I guess.

'Then it's a different matter,' the Karen person says. 'That would represent another stage in the disciplinary process. We would be further down the line.'

I was right.

'Yes, let's keep it verbal just now, shall we,' says the Dean, 'and try to sort something out.'

Sort something out. Didn't Mason say this? We can sort something out? He's evidently decided I might as well be hung for a sheep as a lamb. I guess he's got even more to hide now and he's bluffing a shite hand.

'From the beginning,' Mason starts off, as if he were writing the Book of Genesis, 'Madeleine has been difficult, let's just say. I wouldn't put it as strongly as 'unco-operative' but difficult, definitely.'

All eyes are on him as he lists my perceived defects. How I don't publish as much as I should. (He doesn't count conference posters or proceedings, needless to say. He doesn't count publications in 'low impact journals', he doesn't count reports, he doesn't count research that's too 'applied', he doesn't count funding that comes from the Home Office or any government department, only the big research councils. On the teaching side, he doesn't count topic areas that aren't 'core' or at the 'cutting edge' of the discipline. In other words, since I'm not actually him, I'm some sort of defective.)

After he's finished, the Dean makes to speak:

'I've had a close look, you should know, at Madeleine's output and I must say that I can see both sides of the argument here. I would not like to suggest that what Madeleine does is not worthwhile, or that she's not a valued member of the Department.'

I'm becoming dizzy with double negatives.

'We must remember that if she's – sorry, if Madeleine's – if you're doing more teaching than some of your colleagues, as seems to be the case, then you're freeing them up to concentrate on the cutting-edge research that distinguishes your Department. We in the university are all very proud of the fact that the Psychology Department gained a 5* in the last Research Assessment Exercise and though you didn't contribute much directly to that, Madeleine, nevertheless you did have an important part to play in it.'

He looks very pleased with himself. Mason scowls.

'I think we should agree that we are all valued members of the university who contribute in different ways to the fulfilment of our Strategic Plan. We don't need to fall out over this and I would urge you both to come closer together and co-operate. We don't want the students to suffer just because we can't put our differences behind us. These are the people we are answerable to in the end.'

Who's talking about students suffering?

'Dean, I don't think the students are suffering. I'm the one who's suffering. I'm the one who gets…'

'Madeleine, I think we can say,' says Karen, who now knows what line to take, 'I think we can say that things might be a bit different from now on. We do not want you to feel undervalued and I'm sure that Professor Mason doesn't either.'

No, that's right. He just wants me to feel the weight of earth above my coffin.

'What about the harassment?'

'The alleged harassment of you by Professor Mason?'

'The very same.'

'As I've already said, we can't deal with these allegations here,' she asserts. 'This is not why the meeting was set up. We don't have any paper trail on this one. We cannot trade in unfounded accusations. Now if you wish to pursue your complaint, there are set procedures for doing so. I suggest that you meet with one of our harassment officers in the first instance, who will guide you through it.'

They have special people to deal with harassment? People plural? Not just one person, like a little round nun who will tell someone off?

'Let's call this a day,' suggests the Dean. 'I'm sure there'll be no need for further meetings. Of course we have to respect Madeleine's right to pursue the matter but it has to be promulgated according to official procedures. Karen will point you to the correct guidelines, as she's said.'

He stands up and smiles, unabashed at using a big word wrongly. Of course.

'Thank you all for coming,' he finishes. 'I know you're all very busy people and I'm grateful to you for giving up your time.'

18.

The girl rests her head on the desk, her long hair touching a large plastic bottle containing what looks like urine. All the students have bottles of water or juice; some have good luck tokens. The girl in question looks like she's read through the questions and decided she can't manage any of them. The exam has just started and if I intervene too early there's a risk I'll push her into full collapse mode. I'll give her a chance to sort herself out. So I walk past but, in the meantime, at the far end of the hall, the door is opened and a male student is breaking out. He's going at some pace. I signal to the other invigilator what I'm doing and rush out after the student, finally catching up with him in the quadrangle. I consider a rugby tackle but settle for grabbing his arm.

''Scuse me.'

He looks startled.

''Scuse me but can I ask why you're leaving the exam?'

'I can't do it.'

'Have you looked at all the questions?'

He was only in the exam for three minutes.

'I can't answer any of them.'

'Could you not attempt them at all? Just write something? You can get marks even if you just write a little.'

'I don't know anything about any of them.'

'Look, I'm afraid you'll have to come back in anyway. What's your name by the way?'

'David.'

'Well, sorry David, but you have to come back into the exam.'

'How come? What's the point?'

'There's a rule about it. You should know – you're not allowed to leave in the first hour of an exam.'

'That's mad. What's the point? If you don't know anything, why do they make you sit and suffer? Is it punishment?'

'No. There's a perfectly sound reason for it. People are allowed to arrive for up to half an hour after the exam has started so theoretically, you see, someone might take the exam paper out of the exam, meet their pal with the questions, then the pal has time to look up certain key things before they come in and start the exam.'

'That's still mad. Who's going to do that?'

'Believe me, students do things that are a lot more complicated than that. Anyway, I'm not suggesting you are.'

The rain is on and I'm getting cold.

'How come you think you don't know anything anyway?' I go on. 'Did you not go to any lectures?'

'Some.'

'And did you do any studying?'

'A bit. I couldn't get time off my job last week though, and they made me work at the weekend too.'

He's making no attempt to move.

'But you'll have taken in something, just from sitting in the lectures. Did you not look at the overheads on the portal for the ones you missed? Did you not listen to podcasts?'

'Yeah, most of the time.'

'Then I'm sure you'll be able to have a shot at the questions. Look, come on back in and...'

'I'd rather not. It's pointless. I'll still fail even if I do write something. It won't be enough.'

'It might give you some credit towards the second paper tomorrow, though. You could maybe get an overall pass.'

'I don't think so.'

'Look I'm sorry but you'll have to come back with me anyway. Rules are rules and I'm not allowed to let you leave.'

'What would you do if I said no?'

'You know fine I couldn't do a lot. I'm not going to handcuff you or make a citizen's arrest.'

He smiles suddenly.

'Just for you, ok?'

Inside the hall, the other invigilator comes up to me.

'Keep an eye on the one in the front seat, far row to the left. Ophelia.'

I look at her, see the Millais painting. The long wavy hair spinning in the water.

'Oh?'

'She's been out to the loo twice already.'

'In ten minutes? Has she got a medical condition? She didn't say anything beforehand?'

'No. But she must have something or else she's at it. Do you think you could check the toilet now, before anyone goes back in? I mean the cistern and everything.'

'Christ. You're not thinking of Godfather Two, are you?'

'Maybe. But they're more likely to hide notes in their underwear and read them in the loo.'

'So short of strip-searching them there's not a lot we can do. Oh god what's that?'

There's a loud wailing noise from the back of the room. I realise it's the girl who had her head down on the desk at the beginning of the exam. She's not coped after all. She's emitting loud sobs and disconcerting the rest of the room. I can just see the appeals: "I was doing very well until I was distracted by the loud noise of another student crying. Not only did this take up a lot of time during which I was totally unable to write, it also left me so emotionally upset that I was unable to concentrate for the rest of the examination and subsequently was unable to do myself justice. I know that in different circumstances I would have been able to perform much better."

I go up to the distressed student and put my arm round her shoulders, crouching down. Ophelia will have to wait.

'Come on out with me. We'll go for a little walk. Don't worry. It'll be ok. Come on.'

She lets me walk her out of the hall. All eyes are on us but she can't see anything for tears. We pass David and I notice that he's written a whole page already. My colleague is involving the other invigilator in the hall who's looking after about ten students from his department, whichever that might be. He's a small man with glasses, looking the part much more than I am except he's eating a slice of pizza while sitting on a desk looking over his brood.

'Just another old exam,' my colleague whispers as we pass on the way out. 'Same again tomorrow.'

This day isn't improving from the moment I swore at the alarm and shoved it under my pillow. But later my new friend – is he? - Philip from French, calls in to my office. I haven't heard from him since New Year. Part of me has been slightly expecting to, which isn't too strong an expectation.

'Bloody marking, bloody students,' he announces. 'I can't stand the start of term. Do you fancy going for a coffee somewhere?'

So we sit in the coffee shop, winding past the outside tables to the warmth inside. 'How was your party then? Your bit of it, I should say,' I ask him.

'Good. Yes, pretty good. You should have stayed. How was yours?'

We work through the chain of friendships that led him to be there at New Year and find we have several people in common. We're almost related. The girl serving has waved us over to a table and now brings the drinks. Nearly there, she trips, spilling a cup all over my lap. What with my coat and a thick skirt, the coffee has cooled down before it gets to my skin, fortunately. But I'm soaked through.

'I'm so sorry. I'm so sorry Dr Lamb.'

What?

'It would have to be you. How embarrassing. You're my

lecturer. You taught me last term.'

'Really? I'm sorry, I don't recognise you. What year are you in?'

'First.'

There are hundreds of girls in the class, all looking the same.

'Don't worry. I'm not scalded, which would be the worst thing.'

'I'm so embarrassed. I don't know how it happened.'

All of which explains how I end up at Philip's flat which is nearby.

There's all this nonsense people put in personal ads - listening to Radio 4, interested in art galleries, art house films, going to Italy on holiday. Are you, dear reader, the ad goes on, interested in the same things? Because if you are we'll meet up and shag each other senseless. But the criteria are nonsense if there's no chemistry. We'd do better just to sniff each other.

In the bathroom of Philip's flat I've rubbed my skirt down with a towel. There are no signs of a woman around, no makeup, hairpins, talc, prettifying things. Philip has made me the coffee I had to forego earlier and we sit beside each other on the couch since it's easiest. I think it's that anyway. I'm aware of how much taller than me he is and for a moment I let myself enjoy the security of it. His bulk somehow makes me feel safe, even though I know it's irrational.

'Back to marking I'm afraid,' I say when the coffee's finished.

I stand up. It's getting winter dark outside.

'I thought your exam was only this morning?'

'It was but I've got projects to do. Third year handed in this morning. We like to punish them by giving them work over Christmas, you see.'

He has a lot of Christmas cards still on his mantelpiece. There are books piled on the floor as well as bookcases everywhere. Of course. And a couple of guitars leaning against a wall. He decides in the end to stay at home and shows me to the door. It's a big rambling flat and seems to fit this big rambling man.

The next day, invigilating the second part of the exam goes smoothly. No runaways, no incontinents. David, I note however, hasn't turned up, which cancels my rescue fantasy and teaches me not to be silly.

In the afternoon there's a planning meeting for a new postgraduate course in women's studies. We're determining a title and deciding whether men should be accepted on to the course. If they were to be, 'Gender Studies' would fit. And if not, then 'Women's Studies'.

'Are there any other suggestions?' asks the Chair. 'Something that would make us a bit different from all the other masters in Women's Studies about the country?'

I say something about us being an old and venerable institution. Something less lumpen perhaps. They look at me.

'Ladies Studies,' I say.

Only a couple of them laugh. No fucking sense of humour.

19.

Two of them arrive at the start of my office hour, holding their marked exam papers.

'We just wanted to talk to you about our results. We don't understand them.'

'Fine. Have a seat. Tell me your names, will you?'

I hope I can remember them.

'Right, what did you get?'

'We both got Cs.'

'That's not bad. What's wrong?'

'We need an A or B to get in to honours. We don't understand why we didn't get Bs. I thought I would get an A.'

'Did you not get some feedback on the scripts? It *is* my question you're talking about, is it? I tend to write quite a lot when I'm marking.'

'Yes you did. We just don't understand it.'

'Did you do well on my course last term? I'll look at the scripts in a minute but I'm just wondering in broad terms why you feel that you might have got a better mark. What did you get for the other question in this exam, for example?'

'C,' says the one wearing a red scarf.

'What sort of C? Top, middle or what?'

'Bottom one.'

'And what about you, Linda?'

'I'm Holly.'

'Holly. Apologies. What did you get?'

'D.'

'But you both think you should have done much better on my question. Why was that?'

'I knew all the material. I knew it inside out,' says Holly. 'I studied so much for Abnormal and the question I practised came up. I wrote nine pages.'

Am I supposed to weigh the things?

'And,' she goes on, 'I found some stuff myself. Not just stuff you gave us in lectures.'

'That sounds good. I wonder why you didn't get more credit. There must have been some reason.'

'You wrote in the margin that it wasn't relevant.'

'Then you can't get marks for it, I'm afraid. You have to answer the question. But we'll see in a minute. What about you Linda?'

'I knew everything too. I spent more time on your course than all my others put together.'

'That's a shame.'

'And I bought the book,' she says, playing her trump card.

'Let's see then. Who wants to go first?'

Linda hands over her script. There are lots of comments written on it, thank goodness. Good for me.

'Let's just look at the overall comment at the end: "Too much that's not relevant. Fair account of the theories themselves but no criticisms at all."

'But I wrote so much.'

'Look, though – I've pointed out that the first six pages aren't relevant.'

'Why not?'

'Because you were asked to give a critical account of theories of anxiety and you've just described symptoms of anxiety.'

'I thought you needed to do that first. Look here, I explained that.'

She points out a sentence: "Before considering theories of anxiety, it's necessary to discuss the symptoms."

'But it's just *you* who said that. Not me. It's *not* necessary if you're not directly asked. That's a pity - you could have spent your time doing a critique of the theories – which would have gone towards answering the question. To be honest, I think you were quite lucky to get a C.'

She looks annoyed but doesn't say any more.

'Can you look at mine?'

Holly hands over her exam booklet.

'OK. Right. You seem to have answered the question up to a point. You do attempt a critique, though actually you've done the same as Linda and gone into all the symptoms first.'

'You don't take marks off for that, do you?'

'No...'

'So why haven't I done better?'

'Look at this here – I've said that you haven't covered all the theories. There are a couple of other ones – you don't mention metacognitive theories, for example.'

'But I did do the others?'

'Only in relation to Generalised Anxiety Disorder. You didn't talk about other types of anxiety.'

'I did but you've just told me I shouldn't have.'

'You *described* them, which you weren't asked to do. But you didn't discuss theories, which you were asked to do.'

'But it was ok on Generalised Anxiety Disorder?'

'Well no, this is wrong, see? I've put a note here. And here's another bit that's wrong.'

'But apart from that...?'

Have they been told from birth how wonderful they are?

I am thirteen. I've arranged to meet a friend, it being a Friday night. I'm in the bathroom getting ready. My mother knocks on the door.

'I won't be a minute,' I say.

'What are you doing?'

'Having a bath.'

'Well let me in.'

'No.'

'Why not?'

'Having a bath is private.'

'Let me in. I need to do the bathroom.'

'No.'

'Madeleine if you don't let me in I'll...'

I keep quiet. I don't even splash the water. As if she would think I'd gone.

'Why won't you let me in? Do you think you're special or what? You're just the same as anyone else you know.'

'I don't care. It's private.'

'Hilary Young has baths with her mother.'

'I'm not Hilary Young and I don't.'

'And where do you think you're going tonight?'

'Elsa's.'

'Are you staying there the whole evening?'

I've not yet learned to lie, even through a door.

'Probably not.'

'Well?'

'We thought we might go to the Court.'

'What's that? It's not a pub, is it?'

"Pub" she says with emphasis.

'Of course not. You know I don't go to pubs. We wouldn't get in anyway.

'I don't know the half of what you do. I never know what you're thinking.'

'Why should you?'

'I discussed everything with my mother.'

I've leaned over in the bath so that I'm covered up as much as possible.

'So what's the Court?' she says.

'It's a sort of disco for young people.'

'What?'

'It's for people my age.'

'Is that the place at the bottom of ...what's that street? I've seen them queuing up outside. A lot of little tarts.'

'They're not. They're just like me and Elsa.'

'You look tarty even in your school uniform. I'm not having my daughter being seen there.'

Elsa's mother always tells her she looks nice even when Elsa isn't so sure herself.

'You won't be there,' I say.

'No and neither will you so you can just forget it. And if you say any more you won't be going out at all.'

'You can't stop me.'

'Just you wait and see. I was hoping,' she tries another tack 'that you'd keep me company. Your Dad isn't coming back till tomorrow.'

'I can't help it if Dad is away on business all the time.'

'But I needn't be on my own. Why don't you get Elsa to come over here and we can keep each other company?'

Dear god I hate her I hate her.

'And hurry up, will you?' she says, more softly.

This of course was the night we ran away. The thing she had to hide from everyone.

20.

We take our sandwiches and soup into the small windowless room that passes for a Staff Club. Once upon a time, university staff were exclusively served in a dining hall by waitresses dressed in black, with frilly white aprons and caps. Now if we go there, we have to jostle in long queues stocked with large, loud youngsters. Two members of staff try to have a discussion, while on a couch beside them a young couple are making out. This is not the cross-fertilisation of ideas that was envisaged. We squeeze into hard seats at the table. When my mobile goes off it's the Home, to tell me that my mother has got a bruise. What happened, I ask. "Just a little fall." Where? How? They don't know. What has she bruised? Her shin. You can hardly see it. No, no need to visit. Nothing to be done.

'My guess is they need to report everything, even the breaking of a nail. Maybe they'll phone to tell me the steam in the bathroom has made her curls come out,' I explain to Tony.

'Will you go to see her anyway?'

'There's no point. She won't remember that she's fallen. She hardly recognises me.'

I squeeze to feel some pity but it doesn't come. Instead, into my head comes an image: she and I are going into a shop, me pushing the pram with my new baby niece.

'Put on your gloves,' she says.

'Put my gloves on? Why on earth? We're just going inside.'

'They'll see you pushing the pram.'

Am I going mad?

'What are you talking about?' I say.

'They'll think it's your baby.'

'That's nice then. What are you on about?'

'They'll see from your ring finger that you're not married. They'll think you've got a baby and aren't married.'

Tony is talking about a school reunion he'd been to the night before.

'I thought you were a fly on the wall sort of person,' I say. 'You'd like to see everything but only through a one-way mirror.'

'I wanted to meet my first French kiss. But she wasn't there. It was interesting though. Most of them have become entrepreneurs. I sat next to Keith Fellows who's made a fortune in property. He could retire already, the bastard. It's all overseas stuff. He sells houses on the coast of Mozambique to people inland who've never seen them.'

'Snake oil.'

'Exactly. He wasn't much impressed by my being an academic.'

'How come?'

'No money. Do you know what he said? "What happened to you? You could have made something of yourself."'

My own reunion had had a different ethos. Business was frowned on at our school, as were Art and Drama. Medicine and teaching were the only professions. A girl in my class who'd worshipped our French teacher had ultimately turned into her. In general, it seemed like plain girls had become glamorous while most of the boys had lost their hair and turned into old men. The school hall, however, smelled the same. You can't describe the smell of buildings and yet each has its own.

At the reunion, as I was inspecting my makeup in the loo, a woman came up to me.

'Hi. I'm not sure you'll remember me,' she says. 'I wasn't one of the stars.'

'I know your face. I'm not sure of your name, though. Sorry. What do you mean, 'not a star'?'

But I knew what she's talking about. How could I forget

the points system? You got credit for being clever, for being a prefect or good at sport, or having a principal part in the school show. Or by being unbelievably beautiful. The ciphers, the indicators were there – the opera score, the braid on the blazer, and a particular book under one's arm.

'I didn't play hockey,' she explained. 'I wasn't a prefect and I wasn't in the school choir. I was nothing.'

And there she was – wife, mother, dentist. Fit at last to be part of the human race. For years after leaving, though, we spent our time counting the virtues of others and of ourselves. Unwritten rules, of course. All of it had to be unpicked in later life, turning out to be as much of a task as learning new things.

The hospital in which Rosie has been committed lies at the end of a long avenue. It's a Victorian asylum built in mock Gothic style. The road is lined with heavy rhododendrons and old lime trees. Mist hangs from the leaves and the winter sun is white and obscured, like a lost moon. In the distance, a cigarette identifies a creature walking towards me but it's only when they're up close that they turn out to be human.

Inside the building, an attempt has been made to disguise long wards as homely units; but I know that downstairs there are still dungeons where inmates used to be chained.

Rosie is sitting on the edge of her bed, not yet dressed though it's the afternoon. She looks crumpled, like a balloon with the air taken out. Her slippers are too worn for a young person. She reacts slowly to my greeting and her voice isn't sharp the way it should be. But she smiles and it's her usual sweet smile, which undoes my anxiousness. She says she's fine and asks about my Christmas. We've had this conversation before.

'My head's sore though.' She puts her hands up to her temples.

'I wonder if it's the pills you're taking,' I suggest.

'It could be. Or maybe it's the shock treatment.'

'So you've started that?'

'I had my first go yesterday.'

'Ah...'

I don't know what to say.

'How was it?' I eventually asked.

'I can hardly remember. I do remember the needle being put in the back of my hand and being wheeled along a corridor. The next thing is I'm waking up feeling woozy in my bed.'

'Has that gone now? Feeling woozy?'

'The tiredness has sort of gone. The tired bit in my head. It's sore, though, like I said. In a sharp sort of way. My body's still tired too. Like puffy or oozy or puree.'

'Are you still getting medication as well?'

'I'm on a cocktail. Huh. Shock, pills, different kinds of pills.'

They would cut into her brain as well, given a chance.

'I suppose it's too early to notice a difference?'

'I don't know what difference I'm supposed to be looking for,' she says. 'I don't know what's supposed to be wrong.'

'They seem to think that you had some strange ideas. Like about the baby.'

She looks vague and doesn't react.

'You remember your miscarriage?'

'I remember it, yes. It seems far away now. Is that why I need all this?' She gestures to the surroundings. 'Just because I had a miscarriage?'

'At one point you didn't think that it had been a ... natural process,' I say. 'You were thinking something more sinister.'

This is a struggle and maybe I should leave well alone.

'I needn't have lost it,' she says. 'They didn't try hard enough. They could have saved it and they didn't.'

'So that's why you thought...?'

'That they'd butchered me? Yes.'

'That can't be true, surely? People don't act like that.'

'Doctors kill' she said. 'A lot of deaths in hospital are caused by treatment, you know. Then there's infection. It's a wonder anyone comes out alive.'

'There's something in that. But truly – about the baby. That's different. They would have done all the testing. I'm sure they would have. Think about it – why wouldn't they? And if there were some madman...'

Oh shit.

'... if there were someone intent on ridding you of the baby, just supposing, they could never have got away with it. There would be too many other people around, witnesses.'

Dear god, what am I getting in to? How I wish I weren't so attached to telling the truth, finding out the truth of things.

'You think?'

'For once I can almost say I know so. Anyway, there was the other thing – about Mason.'

'Being the father? Dr Lamb, he was the father.'

'I was hoping that wasn't true.'

'He hypnotised me.'

Christ what now? Is Mason even more wicked or deranged than I think, or is Rosie really out of touch with reality now?

'He said it was an experiment. I'd said in a tutorial that I wasn't hypnotisable and he bet he could hypnotise me. So he tried and it worked.'

'Hang on. When did he try this? Do you mean there and then?'

'Yes.'

'In front of all the others?'

'Yes.'

'But then he couldn't have... he couldn't have had sex with you then?'

Rosie looks at me not understanding.

'You see what I mean? If the others were there. Did he hypnotise you another time then?'

'No. Just the once.'

'Rosie are you saying that he fathered your child that very day? When you were hypnotised? When all the students were there?'

'I suppose not. It must have been another time.'

'Are you sure there was another time? I mean, you said a minute ago that there wasn't another time. Can you remember?'

'Maybe he sent the others out. Maybe it happened after they'd gone.'

'But you don't remember?'

'Not really. I'm having problems with my memory in general.'

'That'll be the pills I'm sure. It'll come back, surely, when you finish with them.'

'When will that be?'

I wish I'd never said it.

'Why was I brought here?' she goes on. 'Was there anything else? Did I do anything?'

'Do you remember talking to Mason when he wasn't there? The night your Dad got the doctor because you were up in your room talking to yourself.'

'Was that it then? Was that why?'

'Your parents were worried. But it's not usual to talk to people who aren't there.'

Unless it's to god of course, I think, when it's called praying. And if god speaks to us, well that's different. This sounded like my bloody lectures again.

'What have they said to you?' I go on. 'Have they not explained what they think is wrong?'

'I saw a psychiatrist once, just after coming in. I've not seen anyone else since except the nurses. And the people doing the shock treatment. Except I don't remember any of them apart from the anaesthetist.'

'Did he explain anything, the psychiatrist?'

'He said I was having delusions. Thinking that my baby had been cut out of me and so on. And that they would give me some treatment to help with that.'

'Did he go into details with you?'

'I thought he was going to. He seemed to but then when I mentioned Professor Mason he kind of gave up on me. I think he was trying to follow it all but that was kind of the last straw.'

'Did you get to ask questions?'

'I asked what the treatment would be and he went in to a lot of details I didn't understand. I had to sign a consent form. And that was it really. He said he would see me again after my treatment had started.'

She seems tired out. I want to kidnap her, take her away from people who are going to harm her. But I can't. Instead I buy her things from the shop. I want to kiss her goodbye but I can't – I'm her lecturer. I pat her shoulder, tell her I'll be back soon. If I believed in prayer I would do that too. But there's a limit.

On my way out I meet Charlie who's carrying some books. Not textbooks, I'm glad to see. He's as smiley as ever. Wants to have a chat sometime.

'Whenever you're free,' he says. 'There's something I need to talk to you about.'

21.

'It's too late for DNA testing,' he says. 'But do you think they would have done it anyway, routinely, or have kept the foetus, so that it could be done now?'

Charlie's looking serious in a way I've not associated with him.

'I've no idea. I can't really imagine so but that's not to say.'

'I think it might have helped. I'm almost certain it's mine. Was mine.'

'Do *you* think she's delusional, then?'.

'I don't know,' he says. 'I don't know what Mason is capable of. He's got a wife and children, hasn't he?'

'Yes. A really nice wife, by all accounts, and nice children too. They must have got her genes. Having a wife and children is no guarantee of anything of course.'

'I've got a theory about her delusions – if that's what they are. Her father is a very strong character, you know. He completely dominates that family. I think she's spent a lot of time trying to please him – to sort of earn his love. She's always talking about him, even if it's not in good terms all the time. But either way, the idea of him is what dictates her life.'

'So how does that fit in with the delusions?'

'This is rich, isn't it?' he laughs. 'What am I? A geologist.'

'Go on, though.'

'I think she reveres her father. She struggles to please him. If he were more accepting, she wouldn't need to think about him all the time. She would just look after her own interests and be herself. But she can't. So she has to act to please him. At some level, though, she resents this. So there's love and there's aggression. This is very Freudian, isn't it?'

'Mmm. And certainly for a geologist.'

'She projects all this on to Mason, so the bit of her that loves her father – in this needy way, of course- is expressed in this idea of having a baby by him. But the hate comes out in this horror scenario that she makes up, when she talks about the way the baby has been surgically removed from her. The hatred is a sort of reaction formation.'

'For fuck's sake Charlie are you on something?'

The vehemence surprises myself even. He looks hurt.

'Sorry. I'm sorry, Charlie. I didn't mean to be so dismissive but you know, we don't talk about this stuff in Psychology any more. There's never been any evidence for Freud's theories, beguiling as they are.'

'Do you think they are? Beguiling?'

'Wonderful prose. Lovely. Good bedtime read.'

'But it's used in therapy.'

'In some quarters. But there aren't many psychoanalysts around.'

'I saw one once.'

'Saw?'

'I went to one. Because I actually *was* 'on something'.

'Oh.'

I wait for him to say more and he does. It turns out that Charlie's was a derailed in the past by pot, and his well-meaning parents got him a private psychoanalyst rather than have him on a National Health blacklist.

'It helped?'

'Yep. It was good. It stopped me using if that's what you mean. It took a while though. Twice a week for almost a year.'

He got off lightly.

'Was Rosie taking it too? Could that be behind what's happening to her now?'

'Not as far as I know and we were quite good friends then.'

'So we're not any further forward in knowing what's

what. We don't know if Rosie is having delusions about Mason or whether it's real.'

'No. But I still think the baby was mine. And I think she'll come to realise that some time in the future.'

'How do you feel about her being in there and getting all these things done to her?'

'I mind but what's the alternative? Unless you can prove anything with Mason. Or get her some other sort of help if she is talking nonsense.'

'Wouldn't it be nice to have these categories, Charlie? "Talking nonsense"; "a bit upset; "out of touch". Not using diseases to lure innocents into mental hospitals. Not legitimising the therapeutics of misguided practitioners. Sorry. I'm lecturing you.'

'No. It's good. Go on.'

Oh this eager youth makes me feel old.

There are about thirty of us ranged round the tables in our large meeting room. The student representatives are attending – a couple of them diffident, the rest happily taking their place amongst the gods. Mason presides at the top of the table. If we'd been dressed differently it might have been a wedding. Drink would have been good.

He starts off by welcoming a couple of new staff members. I wondered who these people were. I don't get introduced personally anymore when they're being shown around.

'I'd very much like to welcome Andrea Fullerton and Roberto Callino. I hope you'll be very happy here. And very productive,' he quips.

The two newcomers give a half wave, looking around the room rather sheepishly.

'Later on we'll be looking at our accounts for first semester and you'll get an even better idea of the opportunities available to you in the Department. There's a very active research wing here and they are able to take full advantage of the generous funding allocated to conference attendance.

'Freebies,' whispers Tony.

'Shh.'

The last conference I went to, in Hawaii, delegates attended the opening session in their beachwear, disappeared for five days and came back to the final plenary with a healthy tan.

'And two?' Tony goes on. 'Wait a minute, how come there are two buggers? I thought there was only one. There was only one set of application papers in the office for us to look at.'

'I'll be coming back to the new members of staff later but in the meantime, a special thanks to the student representatives for coming. Can we please deal with the student business first before they have to leave us? Can I invite you to submit your comments? What have the students being saying about us? Let's start with first year. Anything?'

'Someone emailed me to say that they didn't understand a word in the Brain lecture.'

The speaker looks like she's got up for clubbing. Her breasts are scarcely concealed and wobble with her indignation.

'What was it that they didn't understand? Was there anything specific? Who was it that delivered the lecture?'

'Matzysack.'

'Ah. Well, we'll look into that. I don't think we can discuss Dr Matzysack when he's not here. Where is he, by the way? Is he around?'

'He's at the VIX conference in Aix,' someone says.

'Right. Well, we'll follow up that one. Is there anything else?'

'Some people were wondering whether we could be given all the lecture summaries before the lectures, so we could follow them more easily?'

'Don't we do that already?'

Mason turns to the first-year tutor.

'We do,' she says, 'though perhaps there are one or two individual lecturers who don't realise. They might not have been told.'

'It's Dr Berlioz,' the student volunteers.

We look around for Marcel. Not there.

'I think Dr Berlioz must be engaged elsewhere.'

'He's in Seattle. The Vision conference,' says the administrator.

'I see. Right. This can be sorted very easily when he comes back.'

'Anything else? Second year?'

'There was something about Dr Berlioz's second year lectures as well but if he's not here...'

The second-year rep. tails off.

'Yes. No worries,' says Mason soothingly. 'You can talk to the second-year tutor in the meantime. Where's the second-year tutor? Not here? This just shows how we need more staff! I believe that there are no representatives from the third and fourth years so if you young people wouldn't mind... Thank you so much for coming, all of you. We always find your contributions invaluable.'

When they've gone, the real business begins. Tony and I are not the only ones surprised by the two appointments: even those from the Management Group seem to be.

'Professor Mason!'

Prof. Baird has sprung to his feet, wound up by having to sit on the news while the students were present.

'Are you really saying that we have two new full-time tenured members of staff?'

'Yes.'

'Not a lecturer and his post-doc or RA?'

'No. A lecturer and a senior lecturer.'

'How can this be? We only advertised for one lecturer. I knew nothing about this.'

'We did only advertise for one,' Mason replies.

'But then it's not possible that we've made another appointment.'

'It is. Yes, I'm sorry but I had to act very quickly on this. I knew that Andrea was possibly going to be available. Her own university was trying to keep her and if we didn't top them we would lose her.'

'You mean you just went ahead and made her an offer? Without advertising the post? Without an interview?'

'I've worked with Andrea for several years and I feel I have a very clear notion of her capabilities. It's an opportunity that we couldn't afford to miss.'

'That's not quite the point, is it?' rejoined Prof. Love. 'The point is, you didn't abide by university regulations about ...'

'Employment regulations in general. It's illegal, frankly.'

This was Elsa, one of the senior women staff. A normally detached, very ambitious woman.

'Does this mean to say that you didn't even discuss it with anyone?' Baird takes up again.

'I discussed it with a couple of people from the Management Group.'

'Who? Why wasn't it discussed with all the senior people? At least all the Professors?' says Love.

'I thought I had consulted sufficiently and, anyway, I had to act quickly. I also discussed it with the Vice-Chancellor.'

Mason throws down his trump card. Love is red in the face now and the other Profs are muttering to each other.

'Bliss is it in this dawn to be a nobody,' says the chap next to me, on the other side of Tony.

'I don't know how you think you can get away with it, I really don't,' Love goes on. 'It contravenes Employment Law, it's totally against the letter and spirit of what the university stands for, as an equal opportunities employer. It's just outrageous, in fact.'

'It's done, in fact,' rejoins Mason. 'It's done and dusted. I am sorry but I really couldn't risk losing the opportunity to make such a significant appointment. And the Vice Chancellor agreed with me.'

If there's been any fallout from the Rosie and the scanner affair, it's not hit him yet. The next speaker is fairly new to the Department.

'It's not surprising,' he says, 'since that's how the Vice Chancellor's wife fetched up in the German Department when *he* arrived in post.'

Nervous titters greet this.

'I don't fancy *his* prospects,' Tony whispers.

When the meeting quietens, Mason takes us through the tabled accounts. As always they're unfathomable. Except that I'm able to make out that there is no mention anywhere of the very large endowment bequeathed to the Department a year ago, the income from which feeds into the Research Committee's budget, paying for the considerable number of trips abroad enjoyed by some members of staff, not least Mason himself.

'What about the Anderson Travel Fund?' I hear myself asking. I've decided to give him some grief, if only to shorten his life for a week and indeed for a brief moment Mason looks discomfited.

'Ah, the Anderson Fund. It's treated differently. The accounts for it are done at source. That is, by the Finance Office itself.'

That makes it all right then.

'But we spend the money,' I say.

'Just a fraction of it. We can't spend the capital – just income from the capital, which is a much lesser sum, you'll appreciate.'

'Yes but we spend it all the same and there's no mention of it here.'

'You want to see the accounts for the Anderson Fund?'

'That's what I'm asking.'

'I'm sure that can be done. Alison...'

He turns to the Departmental administrator.

'Alison, can you make sure please that these are done for the next meeting? Thank you for reminding me, Madeleine.'

Perhaps his life has been shortened for more than a week. Maybe ten days?

22.

'**H**i there. How're you doing?'

I'm picking up my latte from the counter, being reminded of the exam answer which had 'Marlatte' instead of 'Marlatt' for a researcher's name. The speaker's hair still looks dyed and I expect his shoes are still shiny. He's on his own and gestures to the chair opposite. Oh fuck. How had we left things? Had I made it clear or was he supposed to be getting in touch with me or what? It turns out he's been researching his ancestors.

'I go back to 1831 at the moment. It's quite surprising – there are some really interesting characters. Have you ever followed up your family? No?'

He proceeds to tell me about his forebears.

'There was William, who's my great great grandfather. That's on my father's side. I told you about my father, didn't I?'

'You told me about how he died.'

'It was awful. What a terrible day that was.'

He gives me a brief resume.

'William,' he goes on, 'was actually the third William in that generation. The first two Williams died, as they did in those days. They went on using the same name till one of them lived.'

I know this.

'My mother lost three siblings – and that's even more recently,' I say.

'He was the village blacksmith,' he continues, 'but it must have had quite a high status then because he had a good income and could pay for a pew in the church. He had nine children - that survived, that is. There were thirteen to begin with. I don't know what ages the other four were when they died. He was quite a character.'

A bit like yourself then, I don't say.

'All the female children died young but the boys did well and lived till they were quite old – old for those days. Isn't that strange?'

'I expect that the women did most of the work. And of course they would be bearing children.'

'The most important one turned out to be the third eldest. He got to be mayor of the town. They didn't travel much beyond their own village in these times, of course. He was well known for...'

He goes on for five minutes. I gulp down my coffee and it burns my throat.

'I'll need to rush. I'm sorry I've got a meeting. I just sneaked out for a bit of a change of scene.'

'How are you anyway? You've not said what's been happening to you.'

Back in the Department I bump into an unknown woman who's holding a kettle and looking for the kitchen.

'Hello,' she greets me warmly, as if we knew each other. I introduce myself and discover that she's Mason's wife.

'I've heard him mention your name,' she says.

I'm waiting for her smile to stall.

'You've been here a few years, is that right? It's terrible that I've never met you before. We must do something about that. What about coming round to dinner some evening?'

What can I say?

'I'll get Roo to arrange something with you. How will that do?'

Roo? This must be her pet name for Robin. Robin Mason. Not a good name. You need three syllables in your first name, with a surname like that.

'Thank you.'

'I've been so worried about him.'

'Really?'

'He's been under a lot of pressure recently and our doctor's been telling him to take it easy. He has to be careful with his heart, as you know.'

I'm counting on it, I think.

'He's a bit grumpy these days – I'm sure you've noticed! But he's not really like that. He's an old softie. Anyway, I hope to see you sometime soon.'

She breezes out of the room. So, he is not just a cardboard cut-out of a bastard. He has a pet name, and maybe sometimes in the kitchen at home he'll sneak a kiss from the wife who still loves him, looks up to him, from the early times when she was his student, longing for the day when she would graduate so that they could go public; and when at night she would lie in the crook of his arm, still trembling, dying from his long slow kisses, him reading softly to her from Winnie the Pooh after they'd made love that shook her heart.

He's still a bit of shit.

'What does he do?'

This is my mother, years ago, standing at the sink with her back to me. I've only been out once with the boy.

'Nothing.'

'What do you mean, nothing?'

'He's a student.'

'Why didn't you say so?'

'It doesn't count. I'm a student. We're not anything yet.'

'It would mean he's got prospects. What does his father do?'

'I don't know.'

'Does he not talk about his family? Has he got any brothers or sisters?'

'I don't know. Excuse me I've got work to do for tomorrow.'

'You shouldn't have been going out then. Where does he live?'

I ignore this and go off to my bedroom to finish an essay. I work at an old table with a bottom shelf that digs into my shins unless I sit sideways and cross my legs. Sometimes I wind them round each other so hard that it takes a few moments to be able to stand up.

I can stare at the wallpaper, still covered in rabbits and ducks and pussycats. I don't mind it. I told her years ago that I wouldn't, even when I grew up, and I don't.

'Do you want supper?' she shouts up now.

'No. No thanks.'

I check how much longer it is before term starts. I wish I could have stayed on in my digs but I don't have the money. I haven't got a job and besides I've got assignments to do over the vacation. My old landlady, who lives in the house, has let me leave my stuff behind but she's had to put it into a cupboard in the hall and let the room out for the summer. She's been kind to me and would adopt me if possible. She empties the rubbish from my room, which is sad because I'm much more fit than she is. She's a cleaner in a school and gets up at 4-30 in the morning to go to work. In winter the frost is glazing the inside of the windows and it's dark for hours more when she shuffles out of the door to start her shift. She's cheery and doesn't mind doing big smiles which show her missing teeth. She shares the house, and a bed, with her sister – the one who was married for a day and a night and then came home. She doesn't say why. I wonder if it was anything to do with the thick growth of hair on her chin. She's a warm and cheerful person. I don't like finding dark pubic-like hairs in the sink that we share though.

When Elsa and I run away at thirteen after climbing out of the window, we walk through the night till we come to the nearest town. It's only three miles. There's a moon, we start to sing and it's the most exciting time of my life. There are signs of dawn in the sky when we reach the outskirts of the town and find an all-night café. We have no concept of a transport café. We hear the laughter coming from inside even at the edge of the car park.

When we go in, all eyes turn to us and the talk stops. It isn't a big place and it's full. A big sweaty man pulls out an empty chair and motions us over.

'Here, I'll get you another.'

'Bert.'

The woman behind the counter tips her head, looking at him.

'The girls want a cup of tea, Ruth.'

She brings over the pint-sized mugs. They look like chamber pots to us. Big enough to bath a budgie in.

'What are you pair up to?' she asks, planking the teas on the table.

'It's a joke,' says Elsa in a very secure kind of way. 'We're having a little adventure, a bit of a laugh. We'll be back before they've had time for breakfast.'

'I don't think you should do this to your parents,' she says. 'I really don't.'

'It'll be ok. They can handle it,' she says. 'We've both got big brothers – they're used to this sort of thing.'

So this Ruth doesn't phone the police, but then she doesn't know that we're going to go round the lorries in the car park to hitch a lift as far away as possible.

'This one's long-distance,' Elsa calls out later when we've outside.

The cab is high up and there's no one inside. Except that a man's head suddenly appears at the window, giving us a fright.

'Just a minute.'

He turns back and then opens the cab door to let out a young woman who's been in with him.

'Hi,' she says to us.

Her tights are ripped, I notice, as she climbs down. She moves on to the next lorry. She looks our age.

He explains he can take us some four hundred miles and we climb up. It's only when we're on the move that a curtain behind us is drawn open and another man, lying on a makeshift bed, reveals himself.

'Hello girls.'

23.

I froth when I think about the denouement to our adventure. I'm full of it and angry, even though it's years and years later that it's caught up with me again, when Miles phones to say she's in hospital again. Stupidly the coincidence makes me fear that I've caused it to happen. She's fallen again, hitting her head against a hot radiator. The staff in the Home suspect she's had a stroke.

I drive there, trying to counter the bad feelings by remembering the benevolent mother she was when we were young enough to fulfil her expectations. When *I* was young enough.

Outside the hospital a notice forbids loitering while another prohibits smoking. In defiance of this a woman with no legs is parked in her wheelchair underneath, lighting up. Something like a coat stand holds up all her tubes.

Inside, past the busy shops and the reception, it's a long walk to the ward. How do some visitors manage? In the ward, Miles is standing at the end of her bed. I doubt she can see him. She herself is lifeless looking, dressings covering much of her face. Her hands with their black veins rest on the coverlet. I think about placing mine on hers but don't.

Miles and I talk quietly. We try to read her notes from a distance in case we're told off for looking. He's already spoken to one of the doctors.

'We're in for a long haul,' he says. 'I hope you've got your pyjamas.'

When she was still in her own house I'd visited her one time last thing at night. She said goodbye from the bed.

'Why don't you spend the night here?' she said. 'Why don't you just come in here with me?'

And I'd tucked her in, as once upon a time she'd done with me.

Miles says to me now, 'Do you remember Aunt Susan?'

She wasn't our real aunt, just a neighbour, but my mother didn't like us using first names for her friends.

'At least it's not as bad as Aunt Susan,' he says.

That year I'd gone back home for the summer we'd had a visit from two women who couldn't get a reply from Aunt Susan's though they were expected. Did we perhaps have a key? We go to the house. Nothing to see at the front. Round to the back garden to see the windows totally clouded over. Once inside the house, there's no smoke in the hallway though, just the scent of freesias, while the door to the back room with the smoke is closed and stiff.

'You phone the Fire Brigade,' I'd said to my mother.

I knew even then that you don't give oxygen to fire. But that's knowledge and real life is different so I pushed and pushed at the door until it opened a little, just enough for me to realise the impediment is a blackened, unrecognisable figure which has been trying to escape. I turn away and soon the police and ambulance and fire brigade are all there.

I was calm at the time and I suppose things like that matter.

'I think we should use the local place, don't you?' Miles says later in the night.

'For god's sake Miles she's not dead yet.'

I look down hurriedly but there's nothing except a faint movement in her throat.

'I'm just being practical, not mawkish,' he goes on. 'We'll have to think about it sometime and we might as well agree on things while we get the chance.'

'Don't you think it's a bit off? To discuss it over her body before she's gone?'

I'm whispering.

'I know I know. What shall we discuss instead?' he says.

'The transubstantiation of souls? Oh well ok then. She wants 'Abide with me'.'

When our father died the minister came to the house. He asked lots of questions about the family.

'This is my daughter, the university lecturer,' my mother said.

'That's very interesting. What subject? My daughter is studying Law and my son was at university. He's a teacher now. It's maths, his subject. They've been crying out for maths teachers so he's had his pick of schools.'

He made some notes from the information my mother is giving out.

'Don't say much about us at the funeral please,' I asked him. 'My father was a very private man. He didn't like to put the family on display.'

'You'll need to talk about what they've achieved, though,' my mother encouraged the minister. 'It was one of his great satisfactions, how well the children had done. Maddie has always worked so hard,' she explained.

Miles on the other hand has a kind of cleverness that allows him to achieve everything without effort.

'Yes, it's hard work, being clever,' I said.

I left them and went back to the room where my father was still lying, his face uncovered though we've closed his eyes. I worried in case he was lonely and I knew that soon he'll be away forever.

At his funeral, in the middle of the minister's grand words, a phone started up with the William Tell overture. And a woman three rows behind keeled over, causing the minister to leave his post and men in dark suits to come running. She recovered later, we heard. After the ceremony, we went to a nearby hotel which makes its business from funerals, for a sit-down meal.

My mother wouldn't have done less. From the outset she busied herself in the room, greeting people, making sure not to miss anyone out. She was pleased that the minister sat at the top table with us.

'You two sit together,' she said to both. 'You've got the university in common.'

After the food, though, she turned to me:

'Come on, you need to circulate. People will be expecting you to talk to them.'

But it's not a fucking wedding.

The wind is cutting our faces as we brace into it. I pull up my hood to protect my ears. I can't even hear Philip walking behind me on the coastal path. We've not so much as met a dog walker in three miles. When he touches me on the shoulder I jump and he laughs.

'Just a kiss,' he says.

I reach up on tiptoe. It's a soft kiss, his hands on my shoulders.

'Ok,' he says. 'Thank you.'

When we shelter for a while in the ruin at the headland he says

'I could fall for you hook line and sinker, you know.'

'Is there an impediment?'

'Why do you say that?'

'The conditional.'

'Clever clogs.'

Silly bitch I am. He's holding my hand and I look down intently. I look at the sparse hairs on the back of his long fingers and note his even nails. I'm frightened to say any more. But I press against him as we watch the slate sea and the gulls hovering and diving and it's easy to bend into the moment.

24.

' " You might as well be shagging a dead chicken,"' I told him.'

'Mel, Jesus Christ you didn't say that did you?'

'Yeah I'm afraid so. I wish I could take it back, of course, but...' She tails off and looks down at her coffee, spooning the froth from the top while waiting for me to continue.

'What did he say, for god's sake?'

'Nothing. He just got up, put his clothes on and left.'

'You're not blaming him for that, are you? God almighty Mel, is there nothing you wouldn't say?'

'That's far too many negatives for eleven in the morning. Let me put it this way. Yes, I regret saying that and yes, I wouldn't do it again. But he was a total dead pancake. He thought he was really clever but he just knew a lot of facts.'

All these men that Mel has mown down in her life.

'He fancies he's charming but frankly I find him totally charmless now. And he snorted.'

'Drugs?'

I suppose I sound a bit shocked.

'No. He snorted when he laughed. You know? God don't you just hate men who snort like that?'

'I wouldn't know if it was real or just a cipher – the snorting and your reaction. Like...do you remember I gave up Alex because his feet were too big? That wasn't about feet.'

Mel screeches.

'Shut up,' I say. 'It wasn't that either. Don't run away with yourself. But what will Dill think?' I remind her, since the man in question is Dill's cousin who arrived from the States a few weeks ago. The academic who'd caused a little bit of excitement in our group.

'I haven't forgotten about Dill. God knows I don't want to hurt her or offend her. But I wasn't exactly thinking about Dill when I said it, was I? Anyway, I don't think it's the sort of thing he'll go around telling people about, do you? The man's a tube.'

'At least now I understand why I didn't hear from you for a while'.

'Sorry. You know what I'm like.'

'Dill seems generous, you know,' I go on. 'But she's not always, in her heart. I wouldn't tell her about it if she asks.'

'Do you think I would?'

Mel laughs at me.

'Sometimes we do do stupid things, you know. Like talk when we don't mean to. It can just be the context, like it's expected of us or something. Of course people are different – some are naturally tight, others leak.'

'I'm glad I'm just an art teacher,' she says, 'and not burdened with all this thinking. Tell me about your new man. I hear there's someone on the scene. Philip, is it?'

'On the scene – yes, there's Philip. But I don't know how long he'll be there. I don't know why. I've just got a funny feeling about it.'

'That's just you, Maddie. Being negative again. What did I tell you last time?'

'I know. But I think I'm picking up vibes.'

'That's a very technical term for a little girl,' she says. It'll be ley lines next. But are you happy?'

'What? Don't be ridiculous. Are you? What are you doing now, for example?'

'At the moment I'm busy buying things for a life I don't have,' she says. 'Just like you, just like Dill, just like all of us. So I'm going shopping after this. Seriously, how are you anyway?'

'Middling. Five out of ten? Things have been difficult at work. I've got a student who's in some trouble and needs help and I worry about her. My mother's had this accident and stuff –

I think Marcia told you. And I'm fed up being on my own. It's like being a perpetual travel agent.'

'But this Philip?'

'I suppose. I can't count on him though, so I have to stand back a bit. It's difficult making a transition from 'I' to 'we', you know,' I say, realising I sound pompous.

'Throw yourself in girl, go on. Just throw yourself in!'

'And end up like you? Saying to him, 'you might as well be shagg….'?

But I don't get to the end. She starts to batter me with the newspaper.

'Remember,' she says after as we go our separate ways, 'it's all part of life's rich fucking tapestry.'

'Dr Lamb?'

Rosie's voice.

'Rosie! How nice. How are you?'

'Grey with grief at this moment, this very precise moment. But embedded in loneliness.'

'What?'

'I had such a grey dream.'

This is not promising.

'How do you mean?'

'I was in a wood somewhere. I think it was a long time ago, like hundreds of years, and I think I was living there. In the wood. I was sitting at a fire in a clearing with some other women dressed in white shifts.'

I think of the dream about my mother in a white shift. Is it hospital that provokes these shared images?

'The ground was damp – it was very leafy and mossy. Or maybe it was the trees that were mossy. It was all greeny-browny roundy about and no sounds.'

She pauses.

'And…?'

'And…and…'

The pause goes on longer than I can bear.

'What happened in the dream?'

'That was it. There were three other women and they were talking but I couldn't hear what they were saying and it was as if I wasn't there at all. Just looking at us from the outside. Do you know what I mean?'

'Being an observer of yourself? Like you get in meditation?'

'A bit. Except that it felt very, very bad. I was really upset. They were discussing me and planning something. They kept looking at me. And they were throwing tiny little birds on to the fire.'

I shiver in spite of trying to be grown up.

'This was food they were cooking?'

'I don't think so. It was more like a sacrifice.'

'What are you saying to me, Rosie?' Were you...'

It's my turn to pause.

'Thinking they were planning to sacrifice me, do you mean?'

I'm glad she said it herself.

'Harm you in some way,' I admit.

'So you think so too?'

'It's not up to me to think anything Rosie. The point is, this is what *you* thought in your dream. You're just telling me about your dream.'

'But do you think they were?'

'I've no way of knowing. How could I? I suppose logically it's feasible but just about anything else could be possible too.'

'Like what?'

Christ, this is getting difficult.

'Lots of things.'

'Tell me some.'

'They could just have been discussing the new tithe system in the village, the neighbours, the difficulty of getting food, various recipes for small birds...'

I regret this right away. This is no time for joking.

'What do you think?' she presses me.

'Rosie I can't possibly say. How could I say? This is your dream. Does it matter anyway? I see that the sacrifice thing is horrible and really that's what we should consider, no? It's your belief about that, and what it signifies, that matters.'

'Do you think dreams are prophetic?'

'No.'

'It would be all right if they were discussing...'

Her voice peters out.

'Go on.'

'I don't know. I forget what I was going to say.'

'Rosie...'

But I've become aware that the background noises are different from what they should be. Why hadn't I noticed? There are no hospital sounds – no cups rattling, buzzing or bleeps or background voices. No traffic.

'Where are you, Rosie?'

'I'm out. I got a pass.'

'Whereabouts?'

'I'm just out for a walk.'

'But where? Are you in the hospital grounds or what?'

In which case I should hear the hum of cars from the road nearby.

'I took a bus.'

'Where to?'

'Just the country.'

'Are you far away then? What bit of 'country'?'

'At the terminus. I got off at the terminus and then walked.'

'What bus was it?'

'I think it was the 45.'

This would take her well out of town.

'Rosie when are you planning to come back from there? It's still winter, remember. It gets dark quite early.'

'I'll be ok.'

'But you don't want to be out alone in the country in the dark. Are there regular buses back? How late do they go on?'

'Every hour,' she says. 'But I'm not ready to go back. It's just lovely here. I mean, outside my head. I had a funny experience coming here, though.'

'What was that?'

'When I was standing at the bus stop, there were bits of skin floating down in front of me.'

I pause.

'Do you not think that they would be bits of paper, or waste or something that's come off a lorry?'

'No, it was skin,' she says.'

'How do you know? Did you discuss it with other people? Were there others at the bus stop?'

'They thought it was dust.'

'There then, didn't I say?'

'They were wrong. There was blood on one bit that landed on my arm.'

'Rosie,' I say firmly, 'are you really out on a pass? Does the hospital know that you've gone off? Tell me the truth now.'

'I left a note. So they do know.'

'But that's not a pass.'

'No.'

'Rosie I'm worried about you. I think you should be back where it's warm and you're cared for.'

She says nothing.

'Rosie?'

'I think my battery's going.'

For a minute I think she means a battery that powers her as a person then I realise she's talking about her mobile.

'Tell me where you are. I'll come and get you.'

'There's no need. I'm fine. I want to find the place where my dream took place. And besides it's lovely. I can see the hills now that the rain has passed. There's a space of blue under the clouds and there are dark islands in it. I think I'll stay and watch the ...'

'I can't hear you, Rosie. Tell me where you are.'

But there's silence from the other end. God damn it. I

check to see whether I've got Charlie's phone number. I think it would be best to phone him rather than Rosie's mother or the hospital. He would be more likely to know her whereabouts. Or am I denying her mother's right, her place, because I'm forgetting it's not the same relationship as mine? Perhaps I should be contacting the police? There's no answer from Charlie and I decide to phone the hospital. I worry that they'll be heavy handed but they could best mobilise the police. Should I do nothing? Wait and see whether Rosie comes back?

The other hospital I should be phoning is my mother's. I said to Miles I would do it and let him know. In spite of our certainty to the contrary, our mother now seems to be moving towards some sort of recovery. She is nothing if not robust and will probably see me off. I phone Rosie's hospital first.

25.

It takes ten minutes to speak to someone in the hospital who knows Rosie. I take part in the lives of five other people before I can get to the point. The nurse is insufficiently concerned.

'She's been assessed and is not regarded as a danger to herself,' she says confidently. 'As I'm sure you can imagine, she's not a danger to anyone else.'

'How can that be though?'

I don't like to challenge hospital staff, not because they're right but because they're in charge. Best, like Brer Rabbit, to lay low and say nothing.

'I'm sorry?'

The woman's voice turns colder.

'I just mean that since she's a psychiatric patient, you might have concerns if she disappears.'

'Of course we do and we will be informing the police. But the point is, she's been having treatment. She shouldn't be a danger to herself, even if she was when she came in. May I ask, who are you anyway?'

I explain. I'm tempted to add my doctorate but it would be a lie to pretend I was a proper doctor. Besides, I would be found out.

'I need to get some details from you, though,' she says. 'Like where you think she might be, for example. We will be informing the family of course. Is there anyone else we should contact?'

I give her Charlie's number though I would rather tell him myself.

'Don't you worry,' she finishes. 'We'll take charge. You can phone back later if you like, to find out the situation.'

How can you hand over worry? If I can't get Charlie soon, I'll phone Philip and get some company. I'm going out to look for her and to hell with them.

Philip parks the car at the edge of a wood near the bus terminus. The wood covers the lower slopes of a hill which we might have to climb. There is a green hill far away. Sometimes your childhood just rears up and hits you in the face. The refrain hammers my mind and I wonder if it's the Obsessive-Compulsive Disorder defence, the distraction in trivia. Or is it the psychoanalytic thing of projection? Jesus fucking Christ Maddie get out of it. And this is self-regulation, talking to oneself.

There's no sign of another human being, far less a policeman. I'm trying to remember the rule. They're not a missing person until how long after they've gone? Or is there a different tariff for psychiatric patients?

'I don't know if she's here. I just have to look, don't you see?' I say in answer to Philip's question.

Does he understand? I don't have to be rational about this. I don't have to give an account of my theories do I?

'Sorry,' he says. 'Come on.'

He takes my hand and we plunge along one of the pathways visible. It's nearly completely dark but we have a large torch. The beam lights up new shoots in the ground. The snowdrops, the crocuses again. There's a thick smell to the undergrowth. I feel self-conscious about calling out her name, realising at the same time how stupid, how very stupid, this is.

In the end we find her by chance because she's off the pathway. Philip has been sweeping the light from side to side and we could easily have missed her. I want her to cry and be normal but she shows little awareness. She's cold and says she was getting a bit afraid but that it was ok. She's wedged between us on the narrow path as we make our way back. I keep thinking how wet her hair is.

26.

It takes me a few days to calm myself. The worry, the rush to the woods and the aftermath of it all, now seem to have happened to another person or a distant me, like myself as a child. It's made my childhood seem large and close, so that it's been leaning on me and bending my thoughts for days. I'm dislocated. When students come through the door, I think they must want to see someone else. I try to set Philip in this frame but he seems like an outline with no emotional resonance. I can't give him any character that might have emerged from our shared experience because it's left me empty. There's no space for this sort of processing and it makes me feel brittle and lonely. I catch myself looking fondly at the figure that pops up on my computer when I effect an action like printing – as if I were less lonely because of its company. Pathetic. But at least I can tell myself it's stress.

I have a dream that I'm abroad with Philip. I hear a cock crowing outside the room by the sea. We've made love, only it turns out we're in the bedroom of someone else's house. The family come home while we're still there. Philip wants to face up to them, unlock the door and greet them. But what if they call the police, I say. So we run away out a back door and I'm full of fear. Then we're on the dank ground and he is making love again to me and I'm holding his head, pulling at his hair and arching my back. I feel his hands under my hips and then I waken up. It stays with me all day.

I've just spent twenty minutes tracing a journal article online, in response to a request from a student. She complains in her email that she can't find a particular test that's described in an article. I look it up, print it out, read it quickly. You can reconstitute the scale from the information in the article, I find. I start to email her this. I have to explain factor analysis and loadings on factors and all that sort of thing. Now all you have to do, I say, is type out the scale again, perhaps re-ordering the items. I point out how they tell you to use a Likert rating scale to score it. So – it'll just take a bit of your time but you're there, I say.

When I take a closer look at the article, however, I see then that the scale is given in an appendix. I go back to my email. Look, I say – you don't need to type it all out again and line up the rating bit alongside each question. It's all done for you. See pages...

I get a response from her in the afternoon. Oh yeah, she says, thanks I actually got it in the library later. Maybe I would have wasted that twenty minutes filing my nails.

There's also an email from Philip, suggesting a few days break in the Easter vacation. But now I have a meeting with a review student who wants to study the cognitions of paedophiles. She's a cheerful child and I'm wonder why she's not looking at something nice, like art therapy.

My mother's talking to me more lucidly than for a long time. Her physical problems have driven her brain into the past where memories are secure and feelings warm. When she was a child, she is saying, she played at shops out in the garden. The old kind of shop like in the days when people served you. She had to improvise, making bacon out of the rolled peel of an orange quarter, slicing it and wrapping the pieces in a flat leaf for her customers. To weigh potatoes, which were small stones, she placed a ruler over a brick and balanced them against a piece of putty or clay, whichever was serving as her measure that day. Short pieces of string stood in for cigarettes and tea consisted of the dark seeds cast from orange red poppies that grew in abundance.

I can visualise her with her round glasses and long curly hair, sitting on the grass and talking to herself. She would be largely ignored by busy parents, her father working even at weekends and her mother caught up in the whole roundelay of meals and washing and godliness.

'I remember getting a plaster put on my finger,' she is saying. 'It was wonderful to have my mother touching me.'

'Did she kiss it better?'

'She didn't go that far. She held my hand while she washed and dried it and then put on the plaster.'

'It's a wonder you weren't driven to cutting yourself on purpose.'

'I did,' she says. 'I did.'

When I tell Miles later on, he doesn't believe me. And I must say, it rattled all my constructs about her.

'Hello. Is that Dr Lamb? This is the Dean's secretary.'

Doesn't she have a name of her own?

'The Dean has asked me to arrange another meeting. This would be just between him and yourself this time.'

'Yes. Certainly. But can you give me some idea about the reason for it please? Is this to continue the previous business or what?'

'I'm not really at liberty to say.'

'Forgive me but is that not rather odd? Usually one can expect to know that sort of thing in advance.'

'I can't really say anything about that.'

I know I should shut up and agree.

'Can you see, though,' I go on, 'that it might be important for me to have some inkling beforehand? Can you not imagine how I might be thinking – let's say – that I am about to get the sack? Just supposing.'

'I'm sure it's not about that.'

'That was just an example.'

'I think it's in connection with your Annual Review.'

'But he won't be conducting it, will he? It's always a

senior member of one's own Department.'

'I don't know. He was quite vague. Anyway, can you tell me whether you would be free Friday, that's a week tomorrow, at 3 o'clock?'

I write it in my diary and note that I have eight days of worrying.

Charlie is waiting outside my office. He's still puffed out after the stairs. I guess that he's remained a smoker after abandoning the more exotic stuff. He's just been to see Rosie – the first time since her disappearance - and he looks older than the last time I saw him.

'I don't know what to do, Dr Lamb.'

'It's ok to call me Madeleine, Charlie. You're not my student, after all. Anyway, on you go. How was Rosie?'

'That's the thing. She seemed really good. She was up and dressed and sounded really bright. Like normal.'

'But did you talk about anything? Anything that might be...let's say, difficult for her. Like her disappearance the other day, for a start.'

'That's why it's weird. She told me about going off from the hospital. Running out of the place. But the way she explained it. . .She said that she was due for another ECT treatment and really didn't fancy it. She felt that if she could be on her own for a bit and get some fresh air – back to nature and all that – that it would do her more good.'

'Did she explain that we had to go and find her?'

'Yes, but she was really low-key about it. Like you'd been out on a walk anyway and bumped into her, almost.'

'It wasn't quite like that I'm afraid.'

'No, maybe not but it was very plausible. What did happen then?'

'I'll tell you in a minute. Can I just ask about the other things? Did she actually mention the baby? Or Mason?'

He hasn't shaved. But he doesn't have a grown-up growth on his chin either. I have a vision of Philip and his dark chin, feeling the texture on my face, liking the scent of the man.

'Like the other stuff, it all sounded reasonable, you would have to say. I did put it to her that I felt bad about the baby too. It's not just the mother who suffers.'

'Did she actually agree that you were the father, this time?'

'I wish. Not just because I would have liked it but because it would have meant that she wasn't fantasising.'

Fantasy is good, delusions bad.

'Has anything been said about when she might get out?'

'She reckons it'll be in a week or two at most. She was almost at the end of her ECT treatments and she thinks they'll let her out just after that. Unless they decide to punish her by giving her some more.'

'Were these her words?'

'She said it but I was thinking it at the same time.'

'What do you feel yourself, Charlie?'

'About her getting out?'

'About whether she's any better or not, really. She wasn't so great when we saw her. Anyway, sorry, what do you think? She's more open with you probably.'

'I don't think she's faking anything if you know what I mean. If she says she's feeling better, I think she really is. And the fact that she's not going on about Mason and that whole story... well, if she were thinking that, she would be saying it too. Do you think?'

'I don't know what to think. The treatment might just have taught her to be more clever and less open. If I were being kept in a place like that and wanted out, I sure as hell wouldn't be using my symptoms in everyday conversation. But then, I suppose we have to give her the benefit of the doubt. That it's true. That the treatment has actually had some positive effect.'

'I can't believe that the process is helping. Electrocuting her.'

'A slight exaggeration, perhaps, Charlie.'

27.

'In the nineteen sixties and seventies, some therapists were even advocating a sexual relationship with 'patients' as part of the therapeutic process. Williams, for example, slept with over thirty of his clients – that's just the ones who came forward later on. Who knows how many more there were.'

Students who've been texting under the table look up. At last I have their full attention. They would be happy to have topics like 'abuse in therapy' every week and nothing, on the other hand, of Visual Perception or Statistics. Sometimes I think that now they've learned to be scientists, they might despise Freud and Jung. But they would love them. Don't believe Freud, I say, but do enjoy him. I forget that we also fell asleep in lectures; were more interested in what the lecturer wore than what they said; loved the human aspect when theory hit real life.

'Excuse me?'

Someone puts up a hand.

'Did he ever get caught? Was he ever punished?'

This is brave, speaking out in front of so many.

'Far from it. He was just being consistent with the values of the time. It wouldn't have been seen as abuse. It took a change in sensibilities before this happened. Attitudes are things of fashion, remember. It's the same with attitudes towards child abuse. Many practices that would now be considered abusive were perfectly acceptable in other times and cultures. Pederasty, for example, in Greco-Roman times.'

Some of them screw up their faces in puzzlement.

'Boy-loving, literally. Anyway, let's look at some figures on abuse in therapy. There's quite an extensive literature on it now. These overheads are up on the portal – have you all got them?'

They nod.

'Right, let's look at this first study.'

I look at the laptop and it's blank. I turn to the screen behind me. Blank except for 'No input is detected.'

Either the connection has gone or the laptop is dead. But it's a new one.

'Just give me a minute please. Does everyone have a copy of the overheads with them?'

We could ignore the screen for their hard copies. Only a few nod now.

'Who doesn't have them?'

About half the class.

'Ok hang on please.'

I never do get it working again. I discover later from Support that the laptop has been set to switch itself off after eight minutes if it's not in use. No one told me. So much for arriving early to set up. I unplug all the leads, remove the memory stick without its permission, realising I may be frying my entire stock of lectures, haul the overhead projector from the floor on to the front desk and pull out my wad of old transparencies. They're in a plastic folder which falls to the floor, scattering the contents. The microphone is out of reach. But then it hadn't been working anyway. Not for the first time I busk it.

'That was very interesting, Dr Lamb.'

She's not looking at me. I lower myself to catch her gaze.

'Good. I'm glad you enjoyed it.'

'The mind is very complex, isn't it?'

'Yes, it is.'

I try not to give her a disparaging look.

'I just wanted to ask you if you thought that that sort of thing still happened nowadays. Abuse in therapy.'

'It does. These studies I was quoting weren't all from

the past you know. There are still regular disciplinary hearings about misconduct in therapists. Inappropriate relations with clients.'

'Really?'

'I'm afraid so.'

'That's very interesting.'

'Is there something particular, maybe, that you wanted to say? Did you have somebody in mind?'

'I've got a friend. She's been seeing a counsellor for four months. I think he's being abusive.'

'Ah. And does she think so?'

She still hasn't looked me in the face.

'Sorry,' I say, 'I'm afraid I don't know your name.'

It's a start.

'So where did you two meet?'

She twirls the glass round in her hand. She has an interesting little bald patch, almost invisible, at the side of her head above the left ear. A blind man running for his life wouldn't notice it. They're childless so it's not the post-natal baldness that Miles's wife had. Trichotillomania, perhaps. That would be a first. Cool. Maybe I could invent an I-spy book for mental disorders. Or am I just inflicting these imaginary problems on her to render her less perfect? This couple with 'mushroom omelette' in French on their dishtowel.

Philip and I are visiting his friends for dinner. We've just finished the first course - a borscht. The deal is, a different wine with each course. This is fine by me. Philip is being careful since he's driving back. They asked us to stay the night but Philip declined without consulting me. Squeamish, I think, about a couple who would inspect the sheets after you'd gone. The husband, Martin, is well-kept and I guess he washes a lot. He's wearing a very white shirt that has been subjected to extreme ironing. The mix of his aftershave, Sue's perfume and mine, all stirred by the heat of the kitchen, makes me want to throw up over the pork loin stuffed with prunes. Which in turn are stuffed with dates. It's like eating a set of Russian dolls.

'This is lovely,' I say.

She smiles. She's charming, reason tells me. What's wrong with you? Why is her voice squeaking in your head like chalk on a blackboard?

'It's my hobby,' she says. 'We're real foodies, aren't we darling? That's what we do together,' she says, turning back to me. 'We cook together.'

Why is Philip friendly with this pair? It's bad enough when people parade their psychopathology, but worse when it's their normality.

'I couldn't believe my luck when I first met Martin,' Sue is going on. 'He knew so much about everything. He was into classical music – which I love too of course. But he was into jazz and climbing and he taught me...oh, just everything. He took me up mountains,' she ends breathlessly.

I'm suspicious of people sharing their thoughts.

'And here I just want someone to take me down the pub,' I say.

'You're Psychology, aren't you?' Martin asks. 'I've got something you might be interested in. They were throwing it out at my last place. One of Bartlett's memory drums.'

'Really? Oh yes.'

'You take Maddie through darling. I'll have a nice chat with Philip.'

These are not people who would ordinarily eat in the kitchen. It's only because they have the proper kitchen kit – the aga, the refectory table, the set of le Creusier pots and casseroles, the cath kidson everything else. I don't get spoon rests, I have to say.

'Here we are.'

Martin is lifting the instrument off the top of a bookshelf in the study next door.

'Lovely.'

The wood feels nice.

'So – you're with old Philip?'

'Well…'

'I only say 'old' because he and I go back a long way. We were both at boarding school – same year even. It's funny that we've both ended up in the same university after all this time.'

'Yes.'

'It's so nice to see him with someone again. I'm sure you know this but last time was rather tricky, if I can put it that way.'

'He told me.'

Did he fuck.

'You seem such a lovely girl. It's great. I want to give you a big hug. I'm so pleased.'

He pulls me so that I'm pressed up against him. This is practically more than I've done with Philip.

'Yes, fine, excuse me.'

I put my elbows in front of my chest and lever him away. He's unabashed. Immediately he puts his hand on my back and runs his finger down my spine.

'I hope you last, you pair. I really hope you last.'

He's still got the smile on his face. How does he do it?

'Pudding darling!'

She calls out from the kitchen. I wonder if she's had Philip pressed up against the wall, her hand on his crotch. Or burning his bum on the aga.

'We were talking about university management,' says Philip when we go back in. 'Sue is just as cynical about it as you and I are, I think.'

So the woman is not just a living meringue.

'Pudding looks lovely,' I say.

28.

I'm hungry. I've had to rush out without breakfast and now I'm hungry. Coffee makes it worse, grumbling my stomach. There's no food in my office and I can't be bothered to go out again. I try the communal fridge but it's empty. Finally I find some chewy indigestion tablets in my bag.

There's an email about our Annual Review. The attachment consists of one page on the process and six on the benefits for the reviewee. How lucky I am. But I really should take heed in case this is what the Dean's meeting is all about. There are forms to be filled in, hideous audits which invite mendacity. There is much in the document about the university's vision. They stopped calling it 'Mission Statement' after the term became discredited through overuse. It was always good, I used to think, for whiling away time in Accident and Emergency.

'The university's vision,' the email says, 'for its human resources strategy comprises a number of key features, seeking amongst them...' (who seeking?) '...high calibre staff demonstrating a prevailing commitment to...' ('prevailing'? Southwest?) '...excellence and continuing professional development, responsive to imaginative managerial interventions, that is skilled and informed, and motivated to take advantage of extensive and varied learning opportunities.'

If necessary, it continues, 'territorial Human Resource Managers will act as facilitators in relation to advice and guidance relating to both the process and also to the design of an appropriated scheme for local use within the Faculty/Division.'

A text from Mel comes through in the evening. 'Check me home latr. If not, ph police. Café Noir now.' When I phone her mobile at eleven thirty, she answers against a background of chatter and laughter.

'Are you at a party?'

'Still Café Noir.'

'Who're you with?'

'Later.'

'You'll tell me later? Or do you mean I should call you later?'

'Both.'

'Right. What time?'

'One.'

'He's nice,' she's saying. 'But of course he could be anything.'

'What possessed you?'

'Fun. It's like going into a sweet shop.'

'Mel these are men. Not sweeties for Christ's sake.'

'Mmm. This one is yummy. I nearly didn't come home.'

'In which case I would have been phoning the police – as you requested remember? And what would I have been saying to them? "My pal, who is perfectly grown up, has not yet come home from Café Noir."'

'I checked up on his degree and he was a student where he said he was.'

'So that's ok then? Students never go on to be bad guys?'

'We've all gone out with men we didn't know.'

'Yes but someone has known them, usually. They're a friend of someone's brother or cousin or whatever. Someone whose workplace we know. Not just someone out of a catalogue.'

'It's not a catalogue.'

'It might as well be. Do you get two for the price of one deals? Mel will you kindly promise to let me know in advance next time? I can't look out for you if I don't know what's going on. Are you drunk?'

She's giggling away.

'Mel, I love you dearly but you're an idiot. Look, go to your frigging bed will you, and I'll speak to you tomorrow.'

Internet dating. I didn't know it was the next stop after the sweet shop.

Two days to go till the meeting with the Dean. It's a constant refrain, a count down like an advent calendar. But now I'm trying to visit my mother in the Home. Ten sixty-six. I punch in the code. The door rejects it. They've obviously changed it. I ring and ring at the bell but don't get entry till some other visitors are leaving. She's not in the lounge where most residents are sleeping. God she's too young for this. Only two of them are actually watching television while the rest just hear it perforce. They all smile back as I search around looking for her. They would like me to come and talk to them. I find her alone, still in the dining room, slumped to the side in her hard chair. She's fast asleep with some macaroni and cheese spilled in her lap.

'Miles and Madeleine! Yes, I remember them.'

'It's Madeleine, mother. It's me.'

'Where's Miles?'

'He was in yesterday.'

'When will he back?'

'Soon.'

'Today?'

'I don't think so mother. Not when I'm coming in today.'

'Why not?'

'There's no need, is there? If one of us visits you?'

She's hanging on to her rotten life while Rosie is trying to throw hers away. I put my hand on hers and it's cold. I fetch another cardigan from her room and put it round her shoulders since it's difficult to feed her arms through the sleeves. She doesn't say anything but watches me intently all the while. The irises in her eyes are opaque. Like an old dog.

"What do you feel have been your successes in the past

year?" I'm at question three in the Annual Review Form. "I've survived." No of course I can't put that. "I contribute significantly to the honours teaching, as well as to the lower levels. My subject area is popular and my options the most heavily subscribed." Unlike some of you other bastards who only have four in the class. Who don't have to mark one hundred and ninety scripts for the final exams.

"I successfully run the final examinations." No one got the wrong feedback about their results last year. No one appealed. The external was pleased.

"Co-authored one paper which appeared in a good journal." I don't say I'm the second author.

"Currently do not have any grants but working on an application. Have been successful in this regard in the past." When does credit run out?

"Invited collaboration with interdisciplinary group, aiming to produce a book and develop a grant application." Should I put down what it's all about? How psychological theory attempts to explain examples of AWOL, such as non-adherence to medical regimes? Failure to take up rights, like free school meals? I start to explain in numbing detail only to find that the box for all my achievements terminates after two lines.

My contribution to the Department? "Much loved by some" seems more like an epitaph. I bet the failure box expands.

'Rosie!'

She comes in after a soft knock on the door. She's wearing a red and black checked jacket which I want to believe signifies a happy state of mind.

'I'm glad I caught you,' she says. 'I thought you might be off at a lecture or something.'

'No, fortunately. Come on in. Have a seat.'

She sits by the window which I close against the draught. It's wonderful to see her there again. Behind her, the hills are clear in the distance, way beyond the city. Mostly they're obscured by fuzzy weather.

'When did you get out?'

'Yesterday. I thought I'd surprise you.'

'How do you feel?'

'Great. I really do.'

Her cheeks are slightly pink.

'What did they say? Do they want to see you again? Are you having to check back with them or go to an outpatient clinic or anything?'

'No. They seem to think that that's it.'

'Do you feel yourself again?'

'Just about. It's pretty odd being back in here again though. I was really scared about bumping into Professor Mason.'

'I feel the same myself. So are you saying that...you think differently now? About the baby and all that?'

'Yes, the bit about him being the father. You know, I just cringe when I think about that. Did he ever get to know?'

'I don't think so. Even if he had, I'm sure he would have had a sympathetic view of it...'

Much as I hate him.

'...because he would know that you were in the hospital and so on. Do you really feel all right?'

There would be such expectation on her to play normal. She looks up to her left when she speaks.

'Yes. Oh yes. I'm just looking forward to the Easter holiday now. I'm going to have a real holiday. My Mum and Dad are taking me off to the sun for a week.'

The Mum and Dad who are so grateful. Who'll never criticise her again, who will love all her boyfriends. Who'll melt if she should hug them. And she'll love them, in turn, because they never thought her to be bad; just mad. So once more we chat about her work, until she says she's going off to meet Charlie. It seems so all right that I can't help but feel doubt.

I'm still saying goodbye as she goes out the door when she's replaced by another, who pushes past her into the room. Same shape, same size. Is there a template somewhere?

'Hi Madeleine!' she says.

She's reached Rosie's seat at the window before I can think who she might be.

'You ok? We've got this meeting. You ok for it?' she says loudly.

'Yes sure. Is it about your critical review?'

It could only be a couple of things so this is not inspired.

'I was wondering if I could change the topic? Would you mind?'

'Take me through it, then. How far had you got with the old one?'

Give me a clue.

'That's the thing. I hadn't really started it so I thought it wouldn't matter too much if I changed it.'

'What were you thinking of doing it on now?'

She adjusts the three gold bands that are slipping down her forehead.

'Bloody things. Sorry. I bought them in a sale yesterday and they're too loose. But bugger it I'm going to wear them anyway.'

Go for it girl.

'I liked your lecture so much yesterday. I thought I would do something on it. It was really interesting. It's the best you've given.'

I'm not sure how to respond to this.

'Abuse prevention programmes for children?'

'Yeah. Do you think that would be all right? I could use some of your stuff but then I could add in some more recent journals and stuff.'

I thought I'd spent quite some preparing for the lecture by "adding in some more recent journals and stuff".

'What's the rule about it? Is it just articles that have come out in the last five years?'

'That's what it says in the handbook. Of course it doesn't mean that anything older is no good. They managed to do perfectly good research six years ago. It's just to stop students being unaware of recent literature.'

'Would be all right to mention some of the old studies you talked about?'

'If they're relevant. And sound, of course. But the bulk of the content should involve more recent material.'

'So how many articles would I need to read?'

'How long is a piece of string?'

'What?'

'You have to mention what you have to mention. If you're doing a very close analysis of the methodology used in key articles dealing with some controversy, then you'll need fewer than you would if you were trying to give a sort of bird's eye view of an area. A big topic like, say, drug treatment of ADHD compared to family behavioural intervention. There you would be doing a broad overview, so it would be a lot of articles. Books as well.'

'How many do you think it should be for my area?'

'What do you think yourself?'

'You mentioned quite a lot of articles yesterday, didn't you? Of course, some were old so I couldn't really use them. Do you think something like eight then?'

I look at her.

'Seven?' she tries again.

'I think you should look around the literature a bit first, to get a better idea of the size and shape of what you're dealing with.'

'My friend's supervisor told her she needed four.'

'Different topics have different requirements.'

'Are the supervisors different too?'

'That's not what determines whether they ask for five articles or ten. It's the area they're working in that decides it. A lot of people in the department are specialising in quite a specific topic area.'

'But you're not?'

'My research is very specific, but I teach over a broad area.'

'What's your research in?'

'I dealt with it in the lecture yesterday.'

'I must have missed it. My mum was texting me. I told her I was in a lecture. She wanted me to go with her to choose a new carpet.'

'It's abuse-prevention programmes for children. The thing I was lecturing on. The topic you want to do for your review. Or like I said, safety skills training, as we prefer to call it.'

'Why's that?'

'As I said, it's because the term 'abuse-prevention' implies that it's mostly up to children to keep themselves safe, which is wrong. Whereas the skills thing suggests... You see what I'm getting at?'

'So do you think six maybe?'

29.

The Dean is seated when I enter. He stands up, gesturing me to the chair in front of his desk. He's not learned the new democratic mode adopted by doctors, of having the patient's chair to the side.

'How nice to see you again, Madeleine,' he starts off.

There's never a reply to this if you can't reciprocate. He pauses a second then continues.

'I wanted an informal chat today. Just to see how you're getting on.'

This man has a multi-million-pound business to run and he's called me in for a chat.

'Fine, thank you.'

'It was quite unfortunate, that last meeting we had, I thought.'

'How do you mean?'

Christ can I not even be grammatical?

'The way it was set up. You know, as a disciplinary thing.'

'It was, though, wasn't it?'

'We only had Professor Mason's submission on that. It was a bit hard on you that it became formalised the way it did.'

He's wearing a very smart suit. He's extremely neat, even for university management. He's an academic, of course, not a manager, but you can see how the heart lies under that suit.

'What was the alternative?'

He ignores this and continues:

'I gather you haven't taken it any further?'

'What particular aspect of things?'

'There are two possibilities, aren't there? There's your

claim of harassment by Professor Mason. You know, that you brought up at the meeting?'

I just look at him and wait.

'Then there was that letter of yours beforehand.'

'Letter?'

'Yes, the one you sent to Human Resources.'

'The one they lost?'

'Yes.'

'So they didn't lose it?'

'How do you mean?' he asks.

My own phrase resonates and I wonder momentarily whether he's nervous too.

'If they'd lost it, how could you know about it?'

'I had been appraised of the situation.'

'Before they lost it?'

'It was a very serious allegation you made in the letter, Madeleine. Someone from HR came to tell me about it quite quickly, I have to say.'

'And then they lost the letter on the way back. Or had they already lost it when they saw you?'

'No. I read the letter.'

'So why did the Karen woman deny that there was a letter, when we had that meeting?'

'Did she actually deny having the letter? Was it not that it was missing from her file? Or that she didn't have a note of the phone call you made to Human Resources? I'm sorry, Madeleine. I've a lot to keep track of in my head you know.'

He's keeping track pretty well. But his face is so shiny. Does his wife use a potato scrubber on him in the morning? I have a sudden vision of homeless guys skippering under the bridges at the river near the city centre. I spelled it out for him:

'She said that we were unable to deal with the content of my letter because there was no evidence of its existence.'

'We should still have acknowledged that you had a grievance against Professor Mason.'

'You did, actually. You said I could take it up with one of

the harassment officers.'

'And have you done that?'

As if he wouldn't have found out.

'No.'

'Are you planning to, may I ask?'

'The thing I was wanting to pursue was not so much the harassment from Professor Mason as the problem I outlined in my letter to HR.'

'Can we talk about that? Just say in your own words what it was all about.'

Whose words might I use?

'I think you know, Dean.'

'Why don't you call me David? We're quite informal here.'

Until you're sent to the salt mines.

'Do tell me,' he continues.

'Professor Mason subjected one of his students to an MRI scan without abiding by the safety strictures. The ethical requirements.'

'That's what I thought. Do you know if the girl ...er, young women...is all right? I take it there weren't any adverse consequences?'

'It's difficult to say. She was pregnant when she went through the scanner, though she didn't know it at the time. The point is, he never applied for ethical approval. He didn't even go through the standard questions on the proforma. If he had, she would have been alerted to the possibility of there being a problem, even if she didn't know that she was pregnant. She could have worked out that she might have been pregnant. It was unforgiveable, what he did.'

'It sounds like it. So has everything been all right with the young woman?'

'No. She lost her baby.'

'Good God. Really? But did they say it was anything to do with the scan?'

'I don't know. I understand they wouldn't rule it out. I'm not sure how one could have.'

'How is she now? Has she recovered? It's been several weeks...'

He stops. How would he know, if supposedly he didn't know? I look at him closely. He's gazing directly at me now, trying to signal honesty.

'I can work it out from the letter,' he says. 'I know when you sent the letter so I know when the scan was, so I can work out when it would have been that she'd had the spontaneous abortion.'

He doesn't pause.

'What I would like to know is what your feelings are about this now? Obviously we know what's in the letter. Do you want us to take some action?'

Beyond hauling me in for another disciplinary meeting? I decide not to say it.

'Of course.'

'Have you discussed this with anyone?'

'Susan. You know, the union rep?' I remind him.

'I believe she's off work again. It's such a shame. She does seem to have a lot of problems. What about anyone else? Do other people in the Department know about it? Would you say it was common knowledge?'

'Not at all. But I have discussed it with chums.'

'Who would that be?'

'I'd rather not say. Why are you asking me, Dean?'

'David. Please.'

I wait until he continues.

'I've been trying to work through the ramifications of this. We have to take a very broad view on such issues, take all parameters into consideration.'

'Yes?'

'I had a chat with Desmond – the Vice-Chancellor in case you were wondering. I'm sure there are other Desmonds around the university.'

He gives a little laugh. I'm wondering if there are any others in the country.

'He and I were both inclined to the view that we should soft play this one.'

'Cover up?'

'You're a hard woman, Madeleine. That's not the expression I would have used. I don't mean that Mason should get away with it...'

Mason. The gloves are off.

'He would be sanctioned of course. We absolutely can not have that sort of thing happen in the university. It's just not what we're about. We are extremely proud of our research record but we would never compromise ourselves in achieving that. We have standards. Extremely high standards in fact. I know we stand up very well in respect of other Universities too. No. Mason would not get away with it and Desmond and I are in the middle of discussions with HR as to how we'll progress this. I'm taking you totally into my confidence here. Properly speaking, you shouldn't know anything of this and I trust that you will be extremely discreet. But to be honest, I think you deserve to know what we're doing. You are the one who's been – how can I put it? – your trust, your integrity in this matter has been abused.'

'I think the student was the one who was abused.'

'We'll be talking to Rosie too. Take my word for it, we're very concerned about her welfare. We have to see her right.'

Rosie? Rosie? Did I mention her name at any point?

'So,' I say, 'you're not planning on making your response to this public?'

'Not if we can help it. I would like you to see things from the point of view of the university. Can you imagine the damage it might do if this were to become public? At any level? If it got out in the university, it would get into the Press and they would have an absolute field day.'

He's as full of clichés as the Press themselves.

'I know that there has been a degree of negligence. Worse, it might be argued. But it will do no-one any good if we go down the litigation route. I don't think it's something he should end up in jail for, do you? And given that, there's no point in dealing with it other than internally. We can dish out our own punishments. If we went the other way, no one would actually be better off. It couldn't be proved, anyway, that Rosie had lost her baby as a result of Mason's actions, could it? It wouldn't stand up in court.'

'You don't think so?'

'I can assure you. And besides, she would be subjected to a whole lot of publicity that might knock her off balance again.'

He's saying too much.

'We are very proud of you, Madeleine. You were quite right in bringing this to our attention. But we would really like you to trust us now, to deal with it in the way we think best. As I said, we have a very broad view of the whole issue. That isn't to say that we don't identify wrong when we see it, and that appropriate consequences will not be delivered. But it's in no-one's interests to make this a huge thing. It can be dealt with quietly, but effectively if I may say so.'

'It sounds like an abortion.'

He moves back in his chair. Then he smiles.

'That's a bit unfortunate. But you're right. It is a bit like that.'

Outside the building there's an automatic drill going.

'We will not let Rosie suffer, Madeleine, and we'll not let you suffer.'

'What do you mean, you'll not let me suffer?'

'You and I will keep in close touch. I want to be sure that Mason does not impinge negatively on your life anymore. I can assure you that he will leave you well alone in future. You will not find yourself overburdened with lectures, the way it's been up till now. We're very concerned – and I've discussed this with Desmond too, needless to say - that Professor Mason should not in any way prejudice your prospects for promotion in the university. I want you no longer to think of him as your line manager. I will be your line manager in future. I do hope that's all satisfactory, Madeleine, and that we can all move on. What do you say?'

'I say that I will have to think about all this. I'll need to discuss it with someone.'

'By all means do that. Though please be very discreet. Come back and see me next week, just so we know that it can be wrapped up. It would be nice to have it all tucked away before the Easter vacation starts. I believe you're administering the final exams again this year. How's that going?'

I feel as if I've been beaten up by a knitted baseball bat. I look down at my feet. There's a hole in my tights.

30.

The departmental secretary catches me as I pass by.

'Just the person, Madeleine. I was looking for you earlier.'

'I've been around all morning. I was downstairs photocopying, mind you - maybe that was it.'

She hands me a note with a name and phone number.

'He's an advocate. He's asking if you would phone him back when you get a chance. It's urgent.'

Maybe they're like the press who've always got a deadline that's already passed.

'I didn't get the whole story but it's to do with your work on children's safety. I think he's got a particular court case – a client who's been accused of trying to entice children into his car.'

'Great'.

I hope she appreciates this is sarcasm.

'When did he phone exactly?'

'So you'll phone him back, will you?'

She seems excited by the whole thing.

This is a phone call.

'I have a solicitor who needs some help with a client. I understand that your background is in children's safety. Good. My solicitor was wondering whether it's possible that a child could misinterpret a man's actions because their school had just been undergoing safety training about strangers and abduction by strangers.'

'You mean, unwittingly misperceive the situation? Or

deliberately exaggerate it?'

'The former. The situation is, the client is being defended against charges that he tried to abduct three children. He is alleged to have said "Get in the car". Now, is there any possibility that they could have misheard him, because their perceptions were biased on account of the recent safety training?'

This is no fun.

'I don't like to comment on these matters,' I say, 'To be frank, they're always more difficult than they seem at first sight. I keep away from legal involvements, court work, that sort of thing.'

'I can appreciate that, Dr Lamb. Do you have any immediate reaction, though? Off the record of course.'

'I would only say that when children disclose something, it's generally true, and it's always best to proceed on that assumption. I can see that this is a different sort of question, though.'

There is only one logical answer, of course: in *theory* it is entirely possible that the children could have misinterpreted the experience. Anyone this side of the grave could tell him that. But I'm not going to let a solicitor, and by proxy a potential paedophile, borrow my authority on that.

'It wouldn't be your job, you understand,' the advocate is saying, 'to decide whether or not the defendant is guilty of the charges. Just whether the alternative explanation is possible. And there would be a fee, of course.'

'I'm sorry. I just don't want to be involved myself. I could put you on to one or two people who might be willing to help though.'

'They wouldn't have to be actual experts in the area,' he points out.

'So, you're looking...your solicitor, rather, is looking for what? Just a psychologist?'

'Not exactly any psychologist. One who might have some credibility as an expert witness. Perhaps a child psychologist?'

'I know someone who does forensic work privately and

specialises in children.'

'That sounds promising.'

I mention his name and there's a bit of a silence.

'I believe that we already have a report from him.'

'Oh?'

'It was less than helpful, if I can put it that way.'

The guy gave the wrong answer, in other words, I guess.

'Why don't you try another university?' I suggest.

I give him the names of a couple of Departments where they have a number of developmental psychologists. So I do get some credit in the end.

'He's everything I'd hoped for.'

We're in Mel's flat, and Louisa the petite, as we call her, is talking about Mike, the man she met at Christmas time.

'How can you tell? He's not had a chance to take out the rubbish or change nappies.'

'I can extrapolate from how he is now. I think he'd be good at all that.'

'Besides,' Mel chips in on Lou's side, 'it's not about that. Not yet. There has to be another stage before you knuckle under. You have to get to enjoy a bit of it, do you not?'

I can only give a big sigh.

'Do you realise that we'll all at the same juncture? Just met some guy, working it out?' Mel goes on. She's already had most of a bottle of fizzy.

'"Sugar toes",' she says. 'He calls me sugar toes. I think I'll have to marry him.'

'Now I know you've lost your reason,' I say. 'I do hope you're not serious, Mel. And I don't want to know any more thanks.'

Louisa looks slightly sick.

'I would run a mile if someone called me sugar toes,' she says.

'What sort of upbringing or life experience brings you that state?' I ask. 'When you call someone "sugar toes"? Is that all one word, by the way? Or is it hyphenated?'

'What about Philip?' Louisa changes the subject.

'I've met him,' announces Mel. 'He's lovely. If she doesn't want him, I do.'

'You'll meet him soon, Lou. I'm thinking of having a party at the end of term. And we'll get to know your Mike a bit better too. We can even ask him if he's any good with nappies. That'll advance your case, eh? How's your mother, by the way?'

'I finally had a word with her yesterday.'

'Seriously?'

'Yep.'

Louisa's mother loves her too much; or in too warped a fashion.

'What did you say? Did you plan it or was it triggered by something?'

'Both. I'd been thinking about it as you know but then – as always of course- there was this thing.'

'Which was…?'

'Lorna's wedding. You know – the wedding of the year? It's the big deal, I'm afraid. They're doing it by the bible. So – my mother is trying to make me wear a proper bridesmaid's outfit. She says things like "Lorna wants you to fit in." I tell her that I've discussed it with Lorna and Lorna says I must do what I want, short of arriving naked. So when I tell mother this, she says, well of course Lorna would try to please you. She says that they both know how difficult I am. How Lorna is frightened to stand up to me and how she knows Lorna better than me, remember?'

'What did you say,' I ask.

'I told her that Lorna and I have always been straight with each other.'

'So then?'

'So then she says, "Are you implying that you and I don't talk straight to each other?" I told her that she always came at things sideways. Like the dress thing. How she was trying to make out that this was Lorna's wish but it wasn't, I knew that. I knew it was hers. Then she went into this monologue. "Oh darling how can you say that? I've always had you at the centre of my heart. I wouldn't deceive you ever. Don't you know that you're the light of my life? You're my first born. My reason for living. I would do anything for you."'

'A bit hard on your brother and sister, no?' says Mel.

'You would have been proud of me. I stuck to my guns. "You may feel that way," I said to her, "but that doesn't mean to say that you've respected my feelings or my wishes. It's not enough to say you love me when you go on to undermine me and do everything in your power to get what you want out of me." I could see her stop everything at this point. It was like she didn't know whether to cry or hit me. "This makes me so upset, Louisa. If you only knew what I'd done for you over the years, how I've sacrificed myself, how I've put all my hopes and dreams on you..." "That's the problem," I said. "I can't live your hopes and dreams. You have to let me be myself. I have to live my life, not you."'

'Good for you!'

We both rush over and hug her.

'About bloody time too,' says Mel. 'Come on, drink up. We'll sort the world.'

'Actually...,' I start.

I bring them up to date on the Mason thing – they've not heard about my latest meeting with the Dean.

'He's trying to bribe you,' says Louisa. 'That's disgusting.'

'Wait a minute. He's implied it,' Mel points out, 'but not actually said it. Not in a way that he could be got at for.'

'Your grammar's getting as good as mine,' I say. 'I love it.''Besides, Lou, remember that Maddie needs a job. There's no point in totally alienating her employers. Not yet. I don't mean on the big thing about Rosie, of course. Just the bribery thing.'

She suddenly changes tack.

'If you did get married, Maddie, would it be in black or what?'

She's sitting with her legs swung over the edge of the chair, her shoes on the floor. It's a recognised stage in the evening and goes along with the slight change in her voice when she starts to sound more posh. Soon she'll start to talk about teaching English abroad.

'When I was in Bangkok,' she begins. But my mobile rings and I miss the rest as I go out to take the call.

Mel and Louisa, I'm thinking. Grand mal and petit mal. I love them both.

'Hi Miles. Is everything ok?'

In the background I can hear Mel saying:

'I don't know why I've always felt unlovable. But I think it explains me, really.'

31.

We decide that we don't want her taken to hospital. Why induce further dislocation, for what medical advantage? There's nothing they can do for her that they can't do in the Home, except for providing cold linoleum floors and the noise of nurses talking through the night.

When I arrive, Miles and Jen are sitting by her bed, both on the same side. Jen gets up to give me a hug. There are tears in her eyes. I think how complete the pair of them are.

'You've just missed the doctor,' says Miles.

'What did he say?'

'She's on strong antibiotics. She's got pneumonia but it's the result of heart failure. Her lungs are filling up and there's not much that can be done at this stage. She's shutting down.'

'She's had so much wrong. I wonder why they're even treating her.'

'They have to. But he said it was more a case of keeping her comfortable now.'

'I see. So that's it, basically.'

It sounds hard but you have to be clear.

'He wouldn't say anything about how long. Just that it won't be weeks,' he says.

'Days, then?'

'It could be before the weekend. Even in the next day or so.'

'Oh god.'

Ruth is going to come,' he goes on.

Ruth is our cousin.

'Good. That's good. It's good to say your goodbyes.'

What a lot of "goods". They move to let me stand close to her. I lean over, kiss her cheek. Her breath smells sweet, her nightdress fresh. She doesn't so much as stir.

'She was awake when we came in. They were giving her some yoghurt and a drink.'

'Did she recognise you?'

Silly question.

'No but she took a whole pot of yoghurt.'

We take up our positions. Miles and I talk about schooldays – listing the good and bad teachers again. Retelling incidents that don't match. I describe an event; he says it happened to him. Such are shared memories. We find that the closest accounts tie in with photographs that have fixed the event in both our minds but mostly there aren't any photos and the memories remain fallible.

'You must be fed up with this reminiscing Jen,' I say, as I've done before. But she isn't, which is why everyone likes her.

Twice in the next hour staff arrive in the room. We wait outside while they change her and turn her. The next time it's someone announcing they are the night shift. I take off my boots.

'You look set,' says Miles.

'It sounds as if it might happen tonight.'

'I don't think so. Her breathing is strong. Look, I think Jen and I will pop off now. We've got to get back for the sitter. It's getting near our bedtime anyway.'

He gives a little laugh.

'Just ring us anytime, though, any time at all.'

'Yes,' says Jen. 'It doesn't matter if it's in the middle of the night, remember. Miles will be able to come over. I'll have to stay with the baby of course. But he can be there in five minutes.'

What? So I'm on my own? I don't say this of course. I'll need to think about it.

For two hours I read my book but then start to feel tired in spite of all the coffees the staff have brought. I eat some of the biscuits in the absence of real food. For a while I watch the TV which is tuned to a shopping channel. "The flavour of Etruscan comes back with a vengeance" says the presenter, describing a pair of earrings. I put my boots back on to go to the visitors' toilet along the corridor. There are still residents moving around which is heartening. I thought they drugged them for an early night. As soon as I put the light on, the smell hits me. I notice the brown stuff on the floor first of all, then the sludge dripping down the outside of the bowl. I close the door and go to find a member of staff. When I look back there's already a clutch of them peering in, clucking, going off to fetch things.

The chair next to my mother's bed is comfortable for sitting in but not for actual sleep. I could fain creep in beside her, curling up at the bottom, were I not afraid of waking up to find a corpse beside me. On the far side of her bed, though, I discover a couple of mats propped up against the wall under the window. They turn out to be bed guards which they must use to cushion the metal sides that are put up to stop old people falling out of bed. Like cot bumpers. I note that they think she is past being able to fall out of bed. I place them flat on the floor in the gap between her bed and the window, covering the plastic with a spare blanket I find in the wardrobe.

There are several pillows lying about since they were being used to prop her up. I take one of them and lower myself to the floor. How can it be such bliss, just to stretch out? The blanket on top of me is scratchy. Outside, the corridor is still noisy. God I haven't said goodnight to her. I get up and, leaning over, kiss her carefully on the cheek, avoiding the rough mole on that side of her face. But when I lie down, I start to think about Miles and Jen leaving. How can they, when she may die tonight? They know she's not on her own but do they not want to be present? She was there at his birth, he should be here at her death. It's the deal, it's symmetry.

'Philip?'

Thank goodness he's answering his phone. I ask him what he's doing – it seems too much to dive straight into the scene that I'm playing in.

'I bet you just put them straight into the vase, did you?' I say.

He's bought some roses, thinking I'm going to be coming over the next night.

'What else do you do?'

'You have to cut the end of the stems. Diagonally is best. It's something to do with better absorption of water, they say. Personally I think it's more to give another chance for getting your fingers slashed on the thorns.'

He laughs.

'They also need some food,' I continue. 'If they haven't given you one of these little sachets, just put in a teaspoonful of sugar.'

'You're having me on. Surely? But listen, this is nice to talk to you and all that, but is something up? Your voice sounds a bit hoarse. Are you sickening for something? Do you need to pull out of tomorrow?'

And so I tell him. But no, I don't want him to come. It wouldn't be right somehow and anyway, I will manage on my own. I can call Miles and Jen if I need to. The staff are very good too. They seem to have classed me as one of their charges.

Later I lie and listen to the sound of her breathing. It's so shallow. At times I can't hear her at all and hold my own breath until hers trips in again. Once it disappears for too long and I'm up, leaning over, my hand on her wrist, my eyes checking her neck for the rise and fall. It's there, ever so faintly. The clock says 4-15 a.m. It's now silent in the corridor and still dark outside. For an hour I sit in the chair trying to read, looking up from time to time when the breathing becomes indistinct. I gaze at her worn face, the open mouth with the missing teeth and then turn to the photograph on the bedside table, of her and my father. It was taken in their late twenties, not long before they got married. He is serene; she looks radiant.

The staff come in every hour to prop her up, spoon in the antibiotic and some liquid, and turn her. She rouses when they call her name into her ear, and her eyes open but they don't register anything. They're pale and no longer translucent; they're like opals. They used to scare me, her eyes, when she was angry. You would think that to check for physical threat you might look at someone's fists, or their posture, but it can all be read in the eyes.

I'm eight and have just returned from ballet lessons. I've not been going long enough to get the costume, though I have shoes that belonged to the daughter of my mother's friend. It had all been my mother's idea. I never saw myself as a ballerina. This was a fault on my part, I believe. She was of the view that children were to be worked on, not that they unfolded.

In the dancing class, we have to set the feet apart, stretch out our arms above our heads to the right, keeping them together, and slowly raise our gaze to them. My nails are bitten. We lower the arms slowly, transfer the weight on our feet and repeat the movement on the other side. The shoes that aren't mine are tight, my feet hurt and I don't see where all this is going.

'You what?'

I'm telling her I've given up.

'How dare you.'

My head withdraws into my shoulders.

'You can go back and tell her you're starting again. I've paid money for this. Don't you understand? I've had to pay for ten lessons in advance.'

'But that's not fair.'

'Fair has nothing to do with it. Who do you think you are that you can just go and give up, without telling me?'

'I'm telling you now.'

Her hand moves as if to hit me but it was a matter of honour for her not to. I never did go back to ballet and through time she forgot about it. Oddly, she didn't bear grudges, unlike myself. And when I did well in some piano competition, she rewarded me by taking me to see Swan Lake.

At half past five there's some faint pink light in the sky. I peek through the curtains, wrapping the edges round my face, and stare past the brick buildings to the distance beyond. There are black trees on the small line of horizon.

At half past seven Miles phones.

'How are you? Is she ok?'

'It's all quiet. The nurses have been in regularly but she's ok. There's not been any change since last night.'

'Did you sleep?'

'Not too bad. I put some mats on the floor.'

'I'll be there soon. Jen can't come yet. The minder's coming over later so she'll pop in then. I can let you out for lunch. You could go to that new place up the road if you like.'

I notice the rash on my arms and chest when I'm getting washed at the sink, one foot raised to keep the faulty door closed. I hope it's the blankets. I go out to the new place for lunch, casting back what might be a final look at my mother who's propped up now with her eyes closed.

It's a pub/diner. I consider three other tables before deciding on one near the window. I haven't started to sip my coffee when the next table is colonised by two families with children. The youngest runs around the room, banging into my table, screaming with joie de vivre. The parents ignore this and ruffle his hair when he returns. I rehearse what I would like to say to them. I read an article in my magazine about a woman who was too fat to have children, then it's time to go back.

Another night goes by with no change, until late afternoon the next day when the staff arrive with her medicine. They prop her up, calling her name. Her face twitches but her eyes don't open.

'Come on now,' they say, as if she just needs cajoling. 'Open up.'

They spoon in the paste.

'She's not taking it,' they say.

I can see that. They've pushed some into the front of her mouth but she's not swallowing. Her mouth stays open, the residue sitting on her lips.

'She can't swallow,' I say.

'No. She can't.'

They wipe her mouth.

'We'll just turn her,' they say. 'Check her.'

I go out and look at the goldfish tank in the entrance hall.

'There, she looks better now. You never know. I've seen people rally.'

I smile back at the girl. You have to give people marks for trying.

At nine forty-five that night I realise her breathing has stopped. You check the time because it might be it. Miles and Jen have gone off home. I lean over her. She is still breathing but it's very low, very. Her face has lost its calm and her hand is reaching out. The veins are black.

'I'm here. It's all right. You're not alone, I'm with you. Maddie is with you. And Miles and Jen have just been here too. You're not on your own.'

I say it over and over and louder.

'You can go. It's all right to go. You're with someone, we're with you. You can go over now.'

What claptrap is this I'm hearing from myself? I'm a complete heathen. But she believes in all that, the ferryman, the forever. I would like to believe in the ferryman too. I would put pennies on her eyes, to pay him for rowing her across the river. I'm in tears, not just at her death. It's my father's death, it's my own, it's the death of the children I don't have. And she's not just my mother. She's the archetypal mother, an extension of the mother I once loved a long time ago, and that mother we search for throughout our lives, to find only splinters of her in mortal form.

I press the buzzer and a nurse comes quickly.

'I think she's going,' I say. 'Can you phone Miles? I think you'd better do it now.'

'Of course.'

She comes over and takes a pulse.

'It's strong. I'm not so sure. But of course we'll phone him.'

I go back to the bed, take her hand in mine again. She clasps me hard, so hard I wouldn't have thought she had the strength. But her face is expressionless.

The nurse comes back.

'He can't come just yet. His wife has taken the car somewhere,' she explains, 'but he'll come as soon as he can.'

In a short while, however, I decide to phone him again. It's been a false alarm, I tell him. I just got panicky.

All through the night I hear the woman next door shouting 'Nurse, Nurse!'

She's new, they tell me.

'That'll be Betty,' they say.

'Nurse, nurse!'

'Betty I've just been to see you. I can't come back yet. I've got other people to see to. You'll need to be patient.'

I check the pink sky again in the morning. Eat the breakfast they bring. She's been restless all night, moving her limbs around. I would have thought her pinned down by the weight of blankets. What is the purpose of all this strength now? In my break at lunch, when Miles comes, I go to the shops in town, look vacantly at things I don't want or need. I buy another magazine, not able to think what books I like. Back in the room I sit by the window. Now her hands are below the cover and she looks like a child put to bed. I no longer need to listen for the soft breaths for they're getting louder. I put down my reading, turn to her. The breaths are rough like pebbles grating together. They stop suddenly and along with her I hold my breath. Then she starts again. Another pause followed by a deep, deep breath that must hurt surely. Her eyes open for the first time in three days. But she can't see me for she's watching something in her mind. It's still light outside but I shut the curtains. I put off the television which has been giving some background noise. And I turn to her and wait. There's no time to get Miles and anyway he doesn't mind. I don't ring the alarm. They would only come.

I don't need to close her eyes in the end. She's done it herself. She always knew what the right thing to do was. The girl pops her head round the door.

'Just checking,' she says.

'I think she's away,' I say.

She disappears and comes back immediately with a nurse. I block the door.

'Just a minute. Can you wait a minute please?'

'We have to see her. We need to check her pulse.'

They say it kindly.

'Not yet. I don't want people fussing round her yet. Please, just some quiet, just let me say goodbye.'

They hesitate. What are they thinking?

'We should…we're supposed to…'

But then the nurse pats my arm.

'We'll come back in a bit.'

'Miles?'

'What is it? Has anything happened?'

'I think you'd better come. She's gone. Just a little while ago.'

There's a silence.

'Miles?'

'Yes?'

'We're orphans now.'

32.

I'm back at my desk after a week. There are two hundred and eighty-four emails which take a whole day to deal with. Some offer condolences but most are from students: "I have been trying to reach you without success for three days now..." I'm torn between saying "close bereavement" and thinking it's none of their bloody business.

Halfway through the morning a boy comes in. His hair is gelled so that it stands straight up from his head. I try to look at his face as he talks.

'You run the final exams don't you?'

'That's right.'

I should recognise him but don't. Perhaps his hair was less distinctive in the past. It's only these characteristics that tag them - 'the girl with the polka dot shoes' - and you have to hope they keep everything the same.

'I was wondering if you could tell me what I need to do to get a first?'

Work very, very hard, I think but don't say.

'If you look at what I got last year,' he goes on, 'would you be able to say?'

'I might not be able to tell you any more than you could work out for yourself. Is it not clear then?

'No. I got two firsts, two uppers and four lowers last year.'

'So you're on the border, then, between upper and lower second. Of course as you know – it says in the handbook – the decision is made on a straight arithmetical mean, so it would depend on the actual marks within these bands. If your uppers were high uppers, or if you had a really low mark for one of the lowers and so on – that would all make a difference. It's a bit difficult to predict just from what you say. I can look it up but I'm not allowed to tell you the actual numbers.'

'Why's that?'

'As it says in the book, it's university policy not to give feedback at that level. You just get given the broad grades for papers.'

'That's silly though.'

'It may or may not be silly. I know they're discussing the matter at the moment, with a view to moving over to the American system. Their policy is to have total transparency and students simply get a transcript of all their marks. It's University Management here who are debating it, I should say. Departments can't do what they like, you appreciate.'

'Yes but the thing is, I know I can do better than that.'

'Students tend to do better in their final year, that's true.'

'But I mean I shouldn't really have got these marks last year.'

He rubs his nose.

'Why is that?'

'I wasn't feeling well. I wasn't performing at my best.'

'Did you submit a medical note?'

'I spoke to Dr Anders and he said it wasn't necessary.'

'Who is Dr Anders?'

'He's my Advisor of Studies.'

'I don't know him. What Department is he?'

'French.'

'Why did he say he didn't think it was necessary?'

'I'd had flu.'

'I would have thought that was reason enough to hand in a medical. I don't understand then. Did you not tell anyone in the Department? Not the secretary?'

'I didn't think it worth it after Dr Anders said not to.'

'Did he give any reason?'

'He said it wasn't relevant.'

'Why not, I wonder?'

'I think he thought there was too big a gap.'

'Between having the flu and sitting the exam, you mean? How big was the gap?'

'Three months.'

'I can see what he was getting at then.'

'But it did affect me.'

'Though not quite in the way it would have, had you had flu when you were actually sitting the exams.'

'No, but I felt really rotten for ages and it spoiled my study plan.'

'James…you said James? James, I can only say that I agree with Dr Anders, though I suppose it might have been prudent to have handed in a note anyway. But it doesn't really look as if you have a strong claim to disadvantage.'

Students have been burgled, raped, knocked down by buses and impaled on railings.

'Look,' I go on, 'I'm sure that what you say is true. These flu things can last a long time and they can leave you quite debilitated. But it's kind of difficult to argue for a direct effect some three months later.'

'So it wouldn't have been considered? At the Examiners' Meeting?'

'It would have been logged. And it might have…'

'You said I didn't have a strong claim?'

'That's right.'

'But I had a claim all the same. Would you say I had a weak claim then?'

'I don't think it would have made any difference.'

'But you said it would have been prudent for Dr Anders to tell me to submit one?'

'If only to avoid this conversation frankly, James.'

Bugger.

'Let me tell you something you may not know,' I continue. 'Even if a student produces a medical certificate, showing a very good medical reason why they performed less than optimally, we still can't just elevate their marks. It's not like we can say to ourselves, "poor student, they've had a bad time. They're sort of on the border so let's give them an upper". All we can do is see whether their performance is significantly worse on one paper, the one where they've been ill or whatever, and then set it aside.'

'How does that work?'

'They're given an average of the other marks, leaving out the bad ones from the affected paper.'

'So there's no chance of an upgrade?'

'We are not an airline. So that's one reason. Another is that you didn't submit any medical evidence. And the final one is that even if you had, it wouldn't have changed anything.'

'I see. Oh well I just thought I'd try. Do you think I could still get a first though?'

'I'll need to have a look at the breakdown of your marks. Maybe it would be better if you came back tomorrow, say, when I've had a chance to think about it.'

'That would be great. Thanks. Er...there's something else though.'

'Yes?'

'I was wondering if you would give me a reference?'

'Oh yes? What's that for?'

'I'm applying for the post-grad teaching thingy.'

Not to teach any future children of mine I hope.

'It's quite a tedious application, I seem to remember,' I say. 'Difficult for you and the referee. I did two or three last year. It was a long form and the screen kept disappearing. I don't know why but they always seem to have trouble with their website. When's the deadline?'

'Seven.'

'Seven March – that's next week. Or do you mean 7 April? I can't remember what month it was submitted last year.'

'Seven tonight.'

'What?'

'Yeah, sorry, it's a bit short notice. I was trying to get you last week but the secretary said you weren't in.'

'I was off, which is different. But you've known since when?'

'I got the form in December.'

'James, I have got meetings all afternoon. I plan to leave the university by six, if not before, because I've got something on this evening. It's now 11-30a.m. What do you think I can do about that?'

'Could you not just do it now?'

33.

The tall guy with the bald head is talking when I enter the room.

'It's awfully dark in here. I can hardly see my papers. So much for new buildings. Maybe they forgot to put the lights in.'

'Is it just me,' I ask, 'or does there not seem to be a light switch even?'

Is it really me again? Do people themselves notice? ('The role of insight in mental disorders. Discuss.')

'We couldn't find it either.'

A woman in a red suit speaks up, someone else I've never seen in my life. So much for this fictive community of scholars. Finally the Chairwoman, Helen, bounces in.

'Ooh dark,' she says. 'Sorry folks.'

'We can't find the light switch.'

'There isn't one. Can anyone see a remote? Someone must have removed it. Scuse me, I'll go and have a look.'

'Didn't this building win some award?'

This is the bald guy again. He does look nice. Why am I checking his ring finger?

'Are we having a presentation then? I thought we were just considering some applications,' I ask.

'It's a son et lumiere,' he says.

Academic jokes start from a low base rate.

'It's the light,' I explain to a newcomer. 'There's no light switch. The lights are worked by a remote.'

I feel like I'm talking to Miles's baby.

There's a smell of warm butter in the room, a mystery

never solved. We look through our papers before Helen gets back, since we haven't had advance sight of these difficult cases. One comes from a whistle-blower, concerned about a colleague sanctioning retrospective data collection from a student. The participants were non-English speaking women from a remote region of Afghanistan, who were probably unable to give informed consent in any form, far less written. At the same time, it's known to the Committee that there is a history of dispute between whistle-blower and impugned colleague, so facts have to be separated from motives. The final twist is that the accused party is Chair of his departmental ethics committee.

Righteous indignation. So sweet.

"For those in peril on the sea..." is what I'm hearing. But Helen is actually talking about the peril of ignoring the Data Protection Act. In the meanwhile, I'm back at the funeral, watching the coffin gliding through the curtains to the furnace. The organist is playing ebulliently now he's on home territory - hymns. 'Songs from the Shows' went badly prior to this but now 'Abide with me' is taken at double time. What would have happened if I'd jumped out and taken his place? There are prescribed ways of behaving badly on all occasions. As the coffin disappears you are allowed to cry out but not scream. You can rest your head on your arms, leaning on the pew, but not throw yourself onto the floor. Leaping up and taking over the organ might not pass muster.

On the way home from the meeting, I pick up a ready meal for one, along with a packet of prepared fruit, fork included. I think about Philip, away at a conference. Going round the shop I feel the sort of self-consciousness that in others I would diagnose as depression. In the end it's just yourself rattling around. Wakening up and going to sleep with yourself.

The home phone goes off as soon as I enter the flat. It's Rosie, sounding very buoyant. I pick up Philippe's postcard from the floor while holding the receiver to my ear.

34.

'**I**'ve been looking at your marks.'

'Yes?'

Marjorie Sweet is in my office two days later, holding a bundle of exam booklets.

'They're very low,' she says.

'Very poor answers.'

'I'm your second marker,' she goes on, 'and I didn't have the same difficulty with them.'

'Can I see again? It's the Diploma ones? I'm afraid I thought they were pretty poor. A combination of low content and illiteracy. In my view. Yes, look at this one. You could read it upside down and get as much sense out of it.'

'I agree they're not great. But they're not that bad, are they?'

'You probably aren't aware of what I give them in lectures. The things that are mentioned in this script here – the really bad one. He – is it a he?- lists three points. That's three points out of fifteen he could have given and that's just from my lectures. They're supposed to do outside reading as well. Most of the other students put in six or seven things as well as other stuff. One of them,' I added, 'even showed evidence of original thought.'

'Could you just take a bit of time to look at them again though, especially that bad fail, please? That's the one I'm really concerned about. If we can't agree on it we'll need to give it to the External. We don't want to involve him unless it's really necessary.'

'What's the problem? Do you really think it's worth a

pass? Sure I'll look at them again but it is a post-graduate course after all. I'd be unhappy getting some of this from a first year.'

'It's just a Diploma.'

'It's still a post-graduate qualification.'

'The student's under a lot of pressure.'

'He can submit medical evidence, then, and get it taken into consideration.'

'It's not quite like that. It's to do with his government. There's a lot of pressure on him to succeed.'

'All students have pressure to succeed. We can't take that into account unless, like I said, it's excessive and they produce...'

'You don't seem to hear what I'm saying Madeleine. This is a student who's been bankrolled by his government and basically will be unable to return home unless he graduates. Moreover, he cannot...'

'So a fail is a pass?'

'Moreover, he cannot afford to stay on in this country to retake his exams, even if the Home Office were to allow it. Sometimes you just have to roll with things, Maddie. I know it's not right. I'm with you on that. But we can't totally screw over some poor bastard just because he's from a different culture.'

'How did he get in?'

'He met the IELTS criterion.'

'I wonder if he sat the test himself?'

'Kindly do not even raise that possibility.'

'Anyway that's just language competence. What about his first degree? What were his references like?'

'They seemed good.'

'Did you actually set sight on them? And did you see his transcripts as well?'

'Yes, it all seemed fine. Well... I did have a slight misgiving about one thing. But there was a lot of pressure from the Chair to admit him.'

'Why don't we just give them the degree when we take the money, and skip the middle bit? I'll look at them again, Marjorie, but honestly I don't imagine I'll suddenly think they're all great or that that one's a pass.'

She looks relieved all the same.

I'm still trying to process the conversation with Rosie the other night.

'I did the home kit thing and it looks blue. At least, I think it does', she said.

'Are you pleased about it?'

'Of course. I've been trying ever since, every since you know…'

She tails off. I don't think she's being coy about the previous pregnancy. I think she's become ashamed of the delusions. Her doctors would call it progress.

'She's done what?'

Louisa is bringing me up to date.

'She's going to phone you later. I just happened to be free to go with her,' she explains.

'Is she all right?'

'She's going to be all right. It's no more than first degree, if it's on the same scale as regular burns.'

'Did they see her right away? I wonder what the triage nurse made of it.'

'No. We had to sit for ages. There were people coming in with bits hanging off them, weapons sticking out of them. Just another day at Casualty. Mind you, I think the nurse might have been punishing her too.'

'What impelled her to do it, do you think?' I ask.

'She said it was this new guy.'

'Jeezoh. If he'd asked her to shave her head, would she have done it?'

'You know Mel.'

'I'll ring her. Or do you think I should wait till she rings me? She must be tired out – I bet she didn't get much sleep.'

'Neither did I.'

Louisa had stayed at Casualty with her.

'Yes, but you don't have the injury as well. What did she use?'

'Just a regular depilatory thing, a cream.'

'And she kept it on too long? How long, as a matter of interest?'

'I think it was over half an hour. But you're only meant to leave it on for three minutes apparently.'

'Did she forget? How can you forget that you're giving yourself a Brazilian for Christ's sake?'

'That was the stupid thing. She just misread the instructions. She didn't have her glasses with her in the bathroom.'

'Did she not feel it painful at the time?'

'It wasn't too bad while the stuff was on. Just after she'd taken it off and was walking about.'

'Poor Mel. She won't be so ready in future to do things to please her man. Jesus.'

'I wouldn't go that far,' says Louisa. 'She'll just pay to get it done properly the next time.'

'If there is a next time. Would it not put you off?'

'The burning bush? You bet.'

'I thought you were a nice person.'

35.

Charlie and I are squeezed into the last two seats allocated to eating purposes. It's by sheer chance that we've ended up together but timely, since I've been wanting to speak to him about Rosie's call.

'You're pleased about it then?'

I figure it's best to get to the point.

'Yes. No.'

'I see.'

'Yes, because she seems so pleased. I didn't think she would be up for it yet. But no because it wasn't planned. Not at all. It was just unlucky you know. And it's crazy, isn't it? She's still got a year of studying to go.'

'Will you get much help? Does her mother know?'

'We'll tell her this weekend. I think she'll be upset but not mad, if you know what I mean. They both dote on Rosie and they're so pleased to have her back. But it's silly, after all she's been through.'

'Has she done the test again?'

'No.'

'And it wasn't that clear?'

'So she said.'

'You weren't there then?'

'No.'

'I wonder if it's right? You get false positives, don't you?'

'We'll do it again before we say anything to her parents.'

'Let me know, will you? I must say, all these life events. I can't keep up with you guys.'

'Sure. Can I ask you something different though?'

'Yeah. What's that?'

I'm trying to ignore the student beyond him who's forking fried egg into his mouth while speaking on the phone.

'You know how podcasts? Like your department does podcasts of the first year lectures?'

'Yes?'

'What about DVDs?'

His brother gets DVDs, he explains.

'We do that all the time.'

'His lecture *is* a DVD. He watches it on his own.'

'They're given DVDs instead of lectures?'

'They buy them instead of lectures.'

And it turns out to be a huge amount.

'Who knows then? I daresay there's a committee drawing up plans this very minute. I'd better look to my wardrobe. Maybe I'll claim makeovers on my tax form, being part of the entertainment industry.'

We pick up our trays with the remains of food and slot them into racks at the end of the refectory.

'Maddie have you got a moment?'

Tony appears at the door.

'I've a nice little bit of scandal,' he says.

'Apart from mine, you mean? What now?'

'Marjorie. Marjorie Sweet?'

'Of course. There's only one Marjorie. I was talking to her just the other day.'

'Trouble. Big trouble.'

He rolls out the 'big'.

'Don't tease. What trouble? She's not pregnant is she?'

Marjorie is in her late 40s and I've got pregnancy on the brain.

'Sex and...come on. What's the other?' he asks.

'Sadism?'

'You're warped. But this is quite a good projective technique, isn't it?'

'You should be a psychologist.'

'Sex and money,' he says.

'Ok what bank has she robbed?'

'You mean, whose bank account has she enhanced?'

He comes in and shuts the door.

'I swear I will batter you if you don't get to the point.'

There's only so much tease a person can take.

'You know how our Marjorie's in charge of the Diploma?' he starts to explain.

'I've become acutely aware of that in the last two days.'

'You know how she's in charge of registering them?'

'Fucking yes and fucking get on with it.'

'Fees. Big fees from big overseas. Lots of dosh. Into bank account. Departmental bank account, you ask? No. Big personal account.'

'What?'

'Her own account. Thousands and thousands.'

'What?'

'Is that the only word in your lexicon?'

'How the hell did no one notice?'

'They don't know apparently. The Department, I mean. This is all hush hush. Not a word, not a single word.'

'As if. Is it a reliable source?'

'Next to god himself. But I can't say who.'

'How could the Department not have noticed?'

'The usual suspects – incompetence. Corruption.'

'I can see that Mason would be incompetent. And I know he's corrupt. But with Marjorie?'

'What did I say? Sex and money. Money and sex.'

'You're not saying that he and Marjorie have got something going on?'

'Can't you just see it? Friday nights, after the seminar, her on the desk with her legs in the air? Actually, a desk might be too high for him.'

This image is unfortunately triggered when Mason comes into

my office shortly afterwards.

'May I?'

He gestures towards the chair. I would like to say no but can't.

'What is it?' I ask.

No compunction about sounding ungracious.

'How are things?' he opens.

His solicitousness would be startling if it were genuine.

'I am fine thank you. What is it?' I repeat.

'I want to talk about your teaching.'

Has he heard that I've been lecturing on abuse in therapy? Has he managed to see a link?

'I've been thinking. If you like, I can put someone else on to the first-year lectures,' he says.

'Why would you do that?'

'I was considering your workload. I have to confess that I now see that it's a bit excessive.'

'You mean I wouldn't have to do anything in its place?'

'No such thing as a free lunch, eh?'

He laughs as if we were friends all of a sudden. It's worse than being enemies. I would rather he'd spat.

'It's not so bad, first year,' I say. 'The lectures aren't very demanding.'

'It would certainly be easier for someone to pick up your first-year lectures than your fourth-year ones. You don't need to be an expert to teach first year.'

So I'm an expert on something now?

'I was wondering about Trudy?' he goes on. 'I think it would be quite useful for her career development to get some lecturing experience.'

'Are you thinking I'll hand over my lecture notes, is that it?

So much for all the hours on course development.

'No no. Not at all. I mean, it would be up to you. I'm sure Trudy would be grateful for some guidance, but it's up to you how much you care to give.'

'I don't mind giving her my overheads. The thing is, I don't want to be found low in lectures next year and then be forced to take on a whole new set. How many of the lectures did you have in mind anyway?'

'The whole lot if you like?'

'All three weeks?'

'Yes.'

'Would this be for next year then? I'm due to start after Easter.'

'No, I mean this year. Trudy would have the couple of weeks up till the vacation, and then the vacation itself. I think she would still have another week after that, before she needed to start, no?'

'I still wonder if she could cope.'

'I'll take her off some of the tutorials. They can distribute them round the other Teaching Assistants.'

'OK but could you send me an email about it? I would like a paper trail. Supposing you went off next year or something – I would like it to be recorded so I don't get something else dumped on me.'

He gets up to go, standing on the bit of carpet where he spilled my plant not that long ago. What is the little bastard after? Presumably he's trying to soften me up. Maybe the Dean has been on to him. And I wonder how Trudy will feel.

The last question is answered soon.

'Maddie?'

It's the first-year secretary on the phone.

'Maddie, it's about your lectures. I've been told that you're off them and Trudy is doing them now. Is that right?'

'That was quick.'

'What do you mean?'

'Mason has just left my room. Just this minute. I can't see how he would have had time to go downstairs and tell you.'

'Tell me what?'

'About what you've just said – Trudy taking over the first-year lectures.'

'He didn't. What are you taking about?'

'He's just been in to my room to ask if I'd mind giving them up. So who told you, if he didn't?'

'Trudy.'

'When?'

'The other day. I meant to mention it to you but I forgot.'

Ratbag. Fucking ratbag. So much for asking me. It's a done-fucking –deal.

'And you're surprised?' she asks. 'Silly billy.'

Outside, the sky is just beginning to get dark. There's no wind. No weather, you would want to say, but that's silly. Like me. I set out for a walk, to stop the blood clotting in my brain. Walking ahead are two students.

'You wouldn't get into a lift with him on your own,' one is saying.

I didn't even bother trying to work out which one of the many it might be.

36.

'Why do you drink so much, Mel,' Marcia is asking. We're sprawled around her sitting room.

'Why do you climb a mountain?' she says.

'Because it's there?' I answer.

'Exactly.'

'We're not ganging up on you Mel,' Louisa says. 'God knows, we drink enough ourselves. It's just that you don't seem very happy these days.'

This is news to Mel.

'I'm always happy,' she says, 'except when I've got first degree burns.'

She shifts in her seat, giving a slight grimace.

'Don't be silly,' I say. 'No one is always happy.'

'Just because you've got permanent dysphoria doesn't mean to say that we're all afflicted.'

'No I don't!' I laugh. 'All right I might be the tiniest bit darker than the rest of you. I don't understand sunniness really.'

'What do you think accounts for it?' Marcia asks.

'I can't talk ill of the dead. God knows what I'm going to do now. I've always blamed her for everything.'

'I never understood why it was always your mother you were hard on,' says Louisa. 'I can see it in my case, but do you not think that some of your anger might be towards Miles?'

'How can I blame him?'

'I don't mean you can blame him rationally. It's not his fault. But he was the one who took your mother away from you. She was always comparing you to him and he was always better. Did you not feel angry with him, and jealous?'

'I see what you're getting at but not really. I'm not sure why, either.'

'Maybe you displaced your anger towards him on to your mother?' suggests Marcia.

'Don't give me guilt to contend with too. I can't start to think that all my wrath towards her was misplaced.'

'I don't mean all of it. Just some would do.'

'Alternatively,' says Mel, 'maybe your mother was less accepting of you because you rejected her, rather than the other way round?'

'I didn't know I was such a fucking mess!'

Marcia sees my look.

'I thought you were serious there.'

'It's simple. I was jealous of Miles but then it wasn't his fault. She inflicted it. These things aren't rational, anyway. The fact is, I've always sensed that Miles loved me but I didn't feel that with her. That's the nub of it.'

'I see,' says Mel. 'Yeah, I can see how that would work. Let's go through all our siblings. Maybe we'll find out why I drink too much – in my happy way, of course.'

'You said the other day,' says Louisa, 'that you didn't know why you couldn't believe it when someone said they loved you.'

'I do know though. It's because I don't love myself enough. I know this because I read this sort of stuff in women's magazines. Psychology has got nothing to do with people anyway. We should ignore all this nonsense for unless we're going to do the three times a week bit on the couch, there's no point. Give me repression any day and to hell with Freud.'

'I've only had enough drink to plan your party,' says Mel. 'Not enough to plunder my childhood. We could do everyone's first memory though?'

So I speak about the flashbacks I have about watching a film about the San Francisco earthquake of 1906. Corinthian columns crashing down, huge chasms dividing the main thoroughfare.

'It was really scary."How old were you?' asks Mel.

'Three.'

Quite unaccountably, tears come to my eyes.

'I don't know what brought that on. Losing my childhood. My mother and that. But it's all this other stuff – Mason...'

'Is Philip not a help?'

'He's good to have around in the background. I don't know if I've got that close to him though. Hell let's talk about the party. Possible dates first. I have checked with Philip, in case you wondered. Will you bring your new guy, Mel? Is he still on the go?'

'My Brazilian? So to speak. Do you mean, has he ditched me because sex currently isn't possible?'

'I don't mean that at all you silly fuck. I only asked because you change your men so often. More than some people change their beds. So it is a new one? What has he got that the last one didn't?'

'That hint of sexual menace?' suggests Marcia.

'Fuck off the lot of you.'

Psychoanalysis. Who need it?

37.

He's wearing a knitted hat, denims, and a leather jacket that he's slept in then jumped on. And he's asleep in the front row of my lecture. I've only just started talking and he's asleep already. Perhaps he's left over from the previous hour? When I was a student, we had respect. We would go to the back of the lecture theatre when we planned to sleep.

While I'm addressing the students, there are two janitors and one unknown man in a suit trying to sort out the problem of an alert message that is plastered all over the screen I should be using. The laptop bleeps periodically while the three of them chatter over possibilities and take turns at repeating useless manoeuvres.

The sleeping boy wakens up when his phone goes off. Half my brain is thinking about what I'm saying but the bigger half is watching him.

'Hi.'

He speaks. He actually speaks into it.

'Excuse me. Phones are not allowed in here.'

He looks up. I wait for the apology.

'Where does it say that?' he says.

I switch off the radio mike and walk over to him. I lean forward and talk quietly.

'It doesn't have to say it son. *I'm* saying it.'

'It should say somewhere.'

'Whether it should, or should not, is a matter I don't care to debate at the moment. I am trying to give a lecture. If you had any idea what that entailed, you would not be doing this.'

He looks at me and without a word puts the phone back

in his pocket. By the time I'm back at the podium I'm more angry than when the incident started. I even have time to think this odd. But at least the three men have managed to sort the problem. It's now fifteen minutes into my talking time.

'Let's look at Szasz's ideas now. He thought that people had 'problems in living' rather than mental illnesses. He wasn't against psychiatry as such. In fact he said that he had no problem with psychiatry between consenting adults. However, as we know...'

Before the lecture I've spent half an hour composing emails to colleagues:

"Dear All,

Please do not tell students the actual marks for their reviews. This is part of their summative assessment and as such has to remain confidential in the same way as exam marks. You may think that you are doing your student a favour. They will indeed *perceive* it as a favour from you. But you are not being helpful to the rest of us who abide by the rules. Thank you for your co-operation."

You will sleep with the fishes.

"Martin,

Can you please give the secretary your questions for the final year Perception paper? They were due in ten days ago. As I'm sure you know, they have to be scrutinised by a departmental question committee before going to the External examiner. All of this takes time and we are already in danger of missing the deadline for the printers.

Please put your questions into Karen's drop box by the end of day."

"Dear Tom,

I understand that you believe that you are exempt from providing questions for the Practical exam for the final year. I'm afraid that you misunderstand the situation. I know that last year no-one answered your question but everyone in the Department has to contribute to this exam. I would be grateful if you would supply one by the end of today, so that we can…"

'She says that it was only temporarily in her account.'

Tony on Marjorie Sweet.

'She should know better than that. How can she argue that she was just placing thousands of pounds in her own account in order to transfer them to a university account later one?'

'Of course she should know better. She's a silly bitch. The thing is, she isn't stupid in other ways. She strikes me as being very sharp.'

'What do you think will happen.'

He reckons she'd be offered a package if she were older. As it is, just a rap over the knuckles. Don't be a naughty girl.

'Do you think that's what they'll do with Mason? Let him away with it?'

'They'll claim they've done something. I imagine strong words have been used already. But unless you personally go ahead and make a formal thing about the scanner or about the relationship with Rosie, it would be too easy just to let it go.'

'Do you think he's been shafting Marjorie?'

I'm a bit ashamed at the word as soon as I've used it.

'Do you think he did with Rosie?' Tony comes back.

'I doubt it. She's more or less retracted that but it's difficult to tell with Rosie. It's total *moral* negligence, no doubt about it – through the scanner without informed consent, not checking whether she's pregnant. Sure. But would it stand up in court? No, the only thing we've got a consensus on, with the Suits, is his treatment of me. And we only know that because the Dean and Mason are falling over themselves to be nice to me, to stop me making a formal complaint.'

'And will you?'

'I want to. I would get him kicked out of this place – into orbit, if I could. But I don't know how much it all might backfire on me or how well I could cope. I want to be able to sleep at night again.'

I wish I could summon up the bravery that Elsa and I'd had. Aged thirteen, running away, hitchhiking. What excitement. But then, bravery isn't being foolhardy and failing to see the danger. We simply didn't *feel* afraid. I'm not sure we were so brave later on, though. We'd asked to be dropped off near a youth hostel or the YW, but then we began to see the neon signs.

Rosie's bouncy when she brings in her essay. I'm so pleased she's managed to hand in an assignment.'

'May I ask the outcome?'

'Positive again. We've told my Mum and Dad.'

'Was Charlie with you?'

'Yeah, he's good that way. He's a very supportive guy.'

'I've gathered. Good. It's not going to be very easy.'

'I don't know how much you've done about Mason and all that but it's probably better just to leave it now.'

I'm not so sure.

'Did you put the review through Turnitin?'

'Should I have?'

'All years have to do it now. It's not difficult but the report is supposed to be submitted along with the review. Tell you what, I'll hang on to it for a day or so and you can bring me the output.'

'I might even mail it to you tonight.'

But I tell her not to bother. That I'm planning a quiet night.

But it isn't a quiet night. At two in the morning the phone rings.

'Hello, Dr Lamb?'

It's a male voice but still I think of Rosie right away.

'You don't know me,' the voice goes on. 'I'm a bit concerned.'

'What about? Who's speaking? Is there something wrong with...'

I'm about to say 'Rosie'.

'About you,' the voice buts in.

'Me? What do you mean? Who is this?'

'Your habit of undressing in front of the window. I don't know if you're aware of it. You leave the curtains open.'

'What?'

'People can see you undressing.'

'I don't leave the curtains open. What the hell are you talking about?'

I know I shouldn't get into a discussion. The keep-safe part of my brain remembers this. But when it happens, you deal with the thing on a common-sense basis and I want to argue the case on rational grounds.

'But you do, Dr Lamb. I can prove it.'

'You're talking nonsense.'

'Do photographs tell lies?'

'That's nonsense.'

I need to find another word.

'I have this… difficulty, you see. I've got these photographs and I don't know what to do with them.'

'That's your problem.'

And I hang up.

The next day the police say it's almost certainly a student, and unlikely to do anything. The call can be traced if it comes to that. Keep in touch, they say. But someone has leeched his way into my home. And he knows my name.

38.

When the phone goes again in the middle of the following night, I brace myself to be brief and assertive with my phantom caller. But it's not him.

'Helloooeee. Hello Dr Lamb. Dr Polly Wolly. How're you doing? I just thought I'd see you're ok. You look after me and I look after you. That's fair, isn't it? Actually, it's not, because you look after me much more than I look after you. So that's not fair, isn't it not? Not. Isn't it?'

The voice turns to giggles. Rosie.

'Do you know what time this is, Rosie? What are you doing? Have you been getting drunk?'

No beating about the bush.

'Aha. Well. That's the big question, isn't it?'

'I know it's not my place to tell you off but...'

I risk her hanging up.

'Has something gone wrong?' I go on. 'I'm sure you're not really taking risks. Something must have happened, is that it?'

She's dropped her phone now. I'm straining to hear whether there's someone with her.

'Is Charlie there?'

I shout down the line.

'Hello! Hello!'

It's a few minutes before she comes back on.

'I'm so sorry. I'm really really sorry.'

'What for? It doesn't matter about waking me up. Is Charlie there? Or is there someone with you?'

'Yes.'

'Is it Charlie? Can I speak to him?'

'No. It's not Charlie. It's a...'

There's a long pause.

'It's a mystereee man.'

'Are you in your flat?'

'No.'

'Oh?'

'His flat.'

'Not Charlie's?'

'No.'

She giggles again.

'Oops. Have to go now. Sorry, so sorry. See you soon. Byee.'

The following day I can't reach her on her mobile. I can't ring Charlie needless to say.

But the morning after that there's an envelope in my pigeonhole. It's her review. At least whatever the blip was, it's over. I just hope there's no lasting damage. The Turnitin report she's attached is very short, I note, before putting it aside. I assume that signifies there's been very little plagiarism. It's the long ones that are suspect, as line after line is reproduced, their provenances fully revealed.

'What do you want me to do with this?'

Philip holds up the tray of glasses.

'I think we'll keep them all in the kitchen. I don't know why I put them on trays in the first place. I'm losing it already.'

It's my party to celebrate the end of term. "Come round to play at my bit," we used to say as children. There's an hour to go before the first people are likely to arrive. I'm praying that nobody comes in time. I've still to clean out the bathroom cabinet, concealing things that are private. I've borrowed rugs to cover the light carpet in the bedrooms. Thank goodness for wooden floors elsewhere. If I went to church, I would have a strange litany. Thank you, god, for wooden floors, paracetamol, cobalt blue, the fading of minor scars and the fact that weight can be lost as well as gained.

I've spent hours and hours on the food. Done the big shop, the big cook. But as I tend to assemble food rather than cook meals, it's been a challenge. I've never let on to Philip that evenings on my own I often have a sandwich for dinner. He's being helpful tonight.

The pasta dish I've made in the morning is beginning to smell faintly sour already. I taste it and can't make up my mind. But there would be a gap if I chucked it, so it stays. The bowl is nice, besides. It's just a different aesthetic choice and I'm trusting it doesn't turn out to be a medical one as well.

There are enough bottles of wine not to bother counting, which is a sort of reckoning in itself. At a party I went to once, the wine bottles had all been turned round so that you could only tell whether it was white or red. Next step is soaking off the labels altogether.

It's near start time, the music is on and I'm beginning to worry that no-one will come at all. Mel and Louisa and Marcia will come over again soon, though. It would it be so good to go back to Postman's Knock and Pass the Parcel.

'Coats in here.'

It's April but still cold. Big heavy wool coats are piling up on the bed.

'Hi.'

I know the man but hadn't asked him. He's invited himself, having met some others in the pub. He's Management Studies and Louisa, I remember, went out with him a couple of times a while ago. All I could remember about him was that he had a thing about making dinner for her, but it was always ready meals. She didn't mind, she really didn't. But he would pretend he'd cooked it himself. That's Management Studies for you, I said. Enterprise.

But then I have a finite number of constructs for measuring men which is why they all end up seeming the same. Your lexicon defining your world.

How often do I say, Mel, I love you but for fuck's sake...? The content varies, of course. This time she seems to be all over Philip. He gives a desperate look when I pass by. But he's a grown man. I haven't had enough drink not to take mild offence, but don't have time to process any of this properly, so file it away and move on. Her new man turns up later. He failed to collect her on time so she'd come ahead on her own. Five out of five this time Mel.

'Are you not having one yourself?' Mel's man is kindly asking in my kitchen.

'I had a glass somewhere,' I say. 'There aren't any more clean ones in here.'

What with various gate crashers, the numbers are twice what I expected.

'Let me try to find you one.'

He goes off before I can object. The table of food is a massacre. Someone has put out a cigarette in the pasta bowl which was still half full. Maybe it's a judgement. There's some drink left but it's difficult to audit since there are lots of opened bottles with different amounts.

The mass of the party has ended up in the kitchen, as always, and my back is being pressed against the sink. I feel the wet seeping into my best dress. Air-force blue, shot silk. You can't even wash the bugger.

'Here we are!'

He comes back, holding a glass in the air.

'What do you want in it?'

What is this man playing at? Why isn't he with Mel in the music room where I'd last seen her, dancing around with the girls?

'Why aren't you dancing with Mel?' I ask.

'I was. I've just come out for a drink.'

'That was decent of you to fetch me a glass.'

'How long have you and Mel been friends?' he asks.

'Us? Millions of years. It's the same with all the group. We got together at the same time and just stuck. What about you?'

I'm not asking him about his friends. Men don't have friends. They just have people they know.

'When did you meet Mel?' I ask him.

I don't tell him we can never calculate this since she moves so rapidly.

'Three weeks? Yep. Three weeks.'

What to say?

'That's nice,' I say.

'She's great. She makes me laugh, you know. And of course she's gorgeous.'

'She's wonderful. But then I'm her pal.'

'I'll just go and look for her,' he says, as if reminded.

'Rory, by the way,' he adds, holding out his hand.

'God she's red hot.'

'I beg your pardon?'

'Mel. I couldn't get away from her. It's not predatory. It's nothing you can object to. At all. She just kind of engulfs you. I'm still trying to work out what it is she does.'

'Rubs up against you perhaps?'

'Give me a break, Maddie.'

'I didn't see you moving away earlier.'

'There wasn't anything to move away from.'

'Sorry. I thought I caught a desperate look on your face.'

'Oh then? I wasn't really in to ...I hadn't worked out what was going on.'

'So something was? Going on?'

I don't know now whether I'm serious or not. I wasn't to begin with. Suddenly I'm in the middle of a fight.

'Not in the least. I just wasn't sure. In fact, she was going on about *you*. Saying what a good friend you were.'

'Good. Now would you mind very much doing that bit of carpet? You would think someone had come through here on all fours looking for spaces between the rugs, just so that they could grind pate and cake into them.'

'To change the subject. About Easter. You don't think you'll manage to get away?'

He's down on his knees now, crawling about with a dustpan. Nice bum. No two ways about it. Can this be called a fetish?

39.

'That's not possible!'

I'm looking over the final exam timetable with the secretary. It's just reached her desk.

'They've scheduled that last exam for the 27th of May and we have our Exam Board on the 3rd June?'

'It's just not possible. You're right,' she says.'We'll need to get back to them right away. I bet all the Departments are screwed. What do they expect? Condensing an eight-week exam period into four weeks. Another triumph for top-down management. They don't have a clue, not a clue, what happens on the ground. We should invite the Vice-Chancellor to come along to your office when you're trying to sort out a thousand scripts from an exam, and staff are handing in piles of marking or have to be chased up for stuff that's ten days late. Look at all those Saturday exams. That's a joke.'

'Can you imagine us fielding sixteen staff on a Saturday to invigilate?' she says.

'That many?'

'If you count the Disabilities, yes. There are hordes of them in separate rooms this year. We've got one with a baby due two days after her exam.'

'Maybe we should put something in the handbook. What'll we do about the times though?'

'The Department that shouts loudest...'

'Medicine?'

'Yep. It'll be best if you get HOD to object, rather than you or lowly me.'

'Me ask Mason a favour?'

'It's not a favour to you. It's for the Department.'
So I draft something to hand him.

Crash. The door opens noisily and Emma from the tutorial group walks in.

'Knock will you! Knock!'

I'm surprised at my boldness. If I'd thought at all, I'd have talked myself out of it. She looks slightly abashed.

'Sorry.'

The others follow quickly, taking their usual place. Just like Church when I was a child. "Move over," my mother would say, "that's Mrs Anderson's seat." Once I sat in the wrong pew which was worse, in her eyes, than the time I wandered off during a shopping trip, holding a strange man's hand.

'How's the mini-project going?' I ask, after hearing about their reviews.

'We've met up and done all the statistics.'

Emma's straight in. She goes on to say, we found a correlation between X and Y, while I'm still wondering whether to interrupt and let someone else talk.

'That's not too surprising.'

I'm still thinking about the stats they've used.

'Why's that?' she asks. 'It's not obvious.'

It comes out like an accusation. She still looks unhappy after my explanation but says nothing. I'm trying to interpret the looks the others are giving her. All this conjecture is tiring.

I've emailed final year about the submission of their projects. Ethics forms have to be submitted separately this year. Now the responses are coming in: "Does this mean that the two are completely separate? It's not that I hand in the ethics form and then you give it back to me and I put it in with our thesis? Or do I put a photocopy in with my thesis?"

I guess life would be half as long without all the repetitions. There are also emails from students about the exams:

"I have heard that the exams will start the first day we come back from the Easter Vacation. Can you please tell me if this is true?"

"No I can't. The timetable has not been finalised. The Department has no responsibility for the timetable, as you've been told. It is entirely in the hands of Registry and you should check their website up until the very day of the exam."

"Why is that?" comes back another email.

"Why is what? What aspect of what I said is causing you to wonder?"

"Why is it that we have to keep checking the Registry website until the day of the exam?"

"Because they reserve the right to change the date or venue of exams at any point in time."

"But that's not fair."

"You are right. It's not fair. But it's outside my control and that's how it is."

Then there are ones that are fishing.

"I've covered X and Y for your lectures. Do you think that'll be enough?"

Why don't you just ask for the questions, I think.

"I have a bad habit of over preparing for exams. I wonder if you could help me by pointing out the chapters that are particularly useful."

Finally, I pull out Rosie's review. The review itself is on top, the plagiarism report underneath. I glance at her Abstract and the first few pages. Splendid. Some flavour of first class. This is wonderful, given all the difficulties. I go to the back for the Turnitin report. Ah. No wonder it was so short. No need at all to match extracts with extant literature. The whole piece has been lifted, in its entirety, from a recent issue of an American journal. How to do a perfect review? Copy a perfect review.

40.

When I'm at the police station it comes back to me. Nowadays the floors are carpeted, there are more signs to read, fewer posters. They're catering for a more literate audience. The officers on the desk smile more. The last time they were mad at me, of course, whereas now they're practising pastoral policing. It should have been more caring the last time. We were only thirteen.

'You say he's been on the phone again? How many times it that altogether?'

The woman officer looks up from my previous report.

'Four.'

'Is it always at the same time?'

'Practically. About five minutes difference.'

'I suppose you've been in touch with the phone company. They can do a lot now.'

'I'm worried because it seems to be someone I know. They know my name.'

'That's why we would like to keep an eye on it too. Have you noticed any of your students being more demanding of your time? Or have you had any approaches from one that you don't know already? Any strange questions in your lecture?'

'A few come up at the end of lectures. They tell you about their friend's bulimia or something. I did have one guy who was a bit strange. When I'd been talking about signs of Child Abuse.'

'Child Abuse?'

'I was pointing them to the lists that practitioners use.'

'What did he say?'

'He asked why there was mention of ears. Marks around

the child's ears.'

'What did you tell him?'

'I said something about erogenous zones. He didn't seem to know the meaning of the word.'

'Has he been back with other questions? Or tried to talk to you at any other time?'

'He came along in my office hour, after that question in the lecture.'

'What did he want?'

'He was asking if I would supervise his project next year.'

'And?'

'I told him it was too early to make a formal choice but that I would take a note of his interest in the meantime.'

'Keen to get you then?'

'I guess so.'

'What did he want to do his project on? Did he say?'

'Some topic in Abnormal. I talked to him about not being able to use clinical participants – patient groups.'

'Did anything seem odd about him?'

But there wasn't. He looked normal. It was just that funny question in class.

This is better than the first time. Me and Elsa, half asleep, slumped on a bench in a police station in London, being made to wait until they could get hold of a woman officer to interview us. It's difficult to know which was worse. Getting stick from her or having to confront our parents when we got home. We fancied being prodigal sons but it didn't work out like that.

Louisa lives in a small, modern flat so that it's like playing in a Wendy house. She's made lovely pasta but then even bread and jam from someone else is great.

'What did he say to you then?'

We have a serious agenda this evening. There's only one item on it and it's called Mike.

'He said stuff about how fond he was of me already, blah blah. You know how they do, before telling you they're just not fond enough of you. So I was thinking all the way through. Not fond enough to go on holiday at Easter? Not fond enough to meet my mother? Not fond enough for our relationship to last beyond dinner? What kind of bloody not fond enough? How many ways am I not fond enough of you? It turns out to be nothing so specific. Just a big general kind of non-commitment not-fond-enough.'

'Did he use the word?'

'The C word? No. It was a bloody game. Spot the meaning in the middle of the circumlocution.'

She doesn't usually swear.

'What makes you think he was curtailing things? Are you sure you haven't misunderstood?'

'I think it was the bit about "I'm not sure where I'll be in a year's time".'

'Ah.'

'And maybe "I don't know how you feel about being exclusive. I have some difficulty with it."'

'I bet he said "It's not you. It's me."'

'How did you guess?'

'What did you say then? Where did you end up? Tell me more about the middle bits. Did he say anything nice, apart from the shit about being fond of you?'

'He tried to. He said I was unique. At least,' she laughs, 'I think that was meant to be good. He said I was the most talented girl he'd ever gone out with. He loved the fact that I played the piano and could speak French.'

'He said "girl"?'

'Bit of a crime, yes.'

'What else?'

I pour some more wine.

'He said things about the stage in life he was at. How his job wasn't secure – he's just on supply.'

'What did you say?

'I kept my dignity. I really like him. That's the trouble -it would be better to stick to people you don't fancy. Maybe it's just because I've sensed he's the one who's going to get away.'

'What did you actually say?'

'I said that if that if he wanted to be non-exclusive, he could be assured that I would be too. But that I would likely decide this wasn't good enough for me. I'm pretty sure that's what I'm going to do – cut him off.'

'Quite right. He's a shit bag.'

'It's just that he's so lovely.'

'Lovely you can find elsewhere, you know that.'

'He's good in bed.'

'You're going to tell me he's the best lover you've ever had.'

'He's the best lover I've ever had.'

'What can I say? Condolences. You'll find another, just as good. Better.'

'He's coming over tomorrow night. I've agreed to make him a meal. Am I stupid?'

'You're not stupid. You're nice. But I think you should serve up our leftovers. There's still some of that nice Italian loaf. It'll be good and stale. And give him something non-alcoholic to drink.'

'Do you not think I should be trying harder to understand him?'

'What is there to understand?'

'How he got to this point. He's probably been let down in the past and won't let himself be hurt again. Maybe I could help him. Teach him something about trust.'

'Or maybe you could just break your heart. Louie lamb don't you see? What's the point? If he's reached this age and still hasn't sorted himself out – do you really think you can do it for him? Especially when he's already doing the spiel about non-commitment?'

'Should I give him an ultimatum?'

'Like, "if you can't commit to me by Saturday I'm going to give you up"?'

'You're right. But it's hard giving up good sex.'

'He can't be the only chemical match in the country.'

'I don't want to have to try them all. Mel maybe, me no.'

'Bless.'

'How about you? I'm sorry, this has all been about me.' She waits for me to answer.

'I'm fine. I don't know where I'm going or what I'm doing – with Philip - but it feels fine. Slightly unreal maybe.'

'How do you mean?'

'He's strong. He's got strong opinions. But I still don't really feel I know him. Not know, in the way I've known previous guys. Maybe I just always knew too much about them. Or felt I knew too much. It was probably a sign that I was bored with them - I thought I could predict what they would think. Probably wrongly.'

'Have you ever been close to getting married?'

'Once. Totally silly. A guy I knew as a student. We got on really well. Maybe too well – a bit like a brother. I did love him in a way, though. One of the flavours of love. I think what I loved was the person he saw in me. But when it came to the crunch, I just couldn't do it. It was great, going out and about and him taking all these photos of me and writing me into scripts for the films he would make. In the end, though, I just didn't want to do it with him.'

'What happened?'

'I'd agreed to marry him. But I said I wanted to keep it secret for a while. How the hell couldn't I have worked that out?'

'And he agreed?'

'Sure. He would have taken me on any terms. You see, I've been a bitch as well.'

'Did you think you wouldn't have been expected to have sex with him or what?'

'I convinced myself that it would come all right in the end somehow. I didn't realise it was important at the time.'

'That's the thing with Mike. It is important.'

'Don't you think you feel it's more important because you know it's going to end?'

'I suppose. Sorry, tell me how it finished with this guy.'

'I met someone else who blew me away and who turned out to be a total shit. I really wanted to have both of them.

'Would two be enough?'

'You realise that we would hate to death any man who talked about women in this way?'

'Total and utter bastard. In fact I'm getting quite angry.'

'And I'm getting thirsty. Here.'

41.

As term draws to a close, students' evaluations of staff are posted on the internal website.

"Madeleine tries hard but it's like following a butterfly."

Ten out of ten for poetry, I'm sure. But the gaps and turns in my thought probably mirrored your micro-sleeps, you little bastard.

"It would be easier if she..."

She has a name.

"...if she put more information on the overheads. She just lists names and dates of studies."

Perhaps I'll post the whole textbook next time.

"Boring. I fell asleep."

"I love Dr Lamb's lectures. She's great. I've finally found the reason I came to university."

I print the page.

'Tony, what am I going to do with Rosie's review? I can't get hold of her. That's three days now and no-one has seen her.'

'Can you take it to HOD?'

'It's not that I need to know the sanctions. I'm thinking about what it means for Rosie. I'd imagined that before the baby came she would at least have a degree.'

'What about her Advisor of Studies?'

'I doubt that he'll know. He's been the one to ask me things on previous occasions.'

'And the boyfriend?"

'I can't. Like I said, she seemed to be with another man

that time she rang me in the night. I suppose I could just ask Charlie if he knew where she was.'

'While I remember, I need to check one of your questions with you.'

'What's the problem?'

'You've used the same phrase twice. It's only a style thing. I've just had the same chat with Mason.'

'What did he say?'

'He said the students would get confused if he put it any other way. The old fart just can't be wrong.'

'It was just a mistake, Dr Lamb. I'm really sorry. I meant to attach my review but I had that article right next to it and must have clicked on it by mistake.'

'You didn't look at the report at all?'

'I was in such a hurry. I thought that when there was hardly anything on Turnitin, it meant that it was ok.'

'The opposite in this case.'

I'm smiling to myself with relief. Rosie's been at Charlie's all along. Neither of us refers to the night call and I begin to think I dreamt it. It's not for me to insist.

'You'll be getting down to swotting now? How does it feel to be nearly finished lectures?'

'Scary. All the others are feeling it worse, though. Rudderless. At least I know what I'll be doing next year.'

I know about the others. I've been writing references solidly: "Good solid upper second-class degree predicted. Works well independently though not averse to taking direction. Highly motivated, diligent and reliable. Good social skills. Relates well to staff as well as peers".

Fits them all.

'Are you still feeling ok?' I ask. 'No sickness or anything?'

'No, great. Thanks.'

'You'll send the right review then?'

It's like spinning plates.

'Does it mean anything, that you don't want to go away at Easter? With me,' he adds unnecessarily.

'My dear man, I would like to but I don't have the time.'

'Why not? What are you doing?'

'Marking final year projects. And a hundred and fifty second year essays.

'But you need some sort of break.'

'We could have the odd day away. If you want to go off for longer, of course, you must. I'm really sorry.'

'Could you be kidding yourself?'

'Philip. What about?'

'Are you sure, in your heart of very hearts, that this is not to do with not being able to spend so much time with me?'

'I'm sure. Sure, I'm sure. How can I prove it? I know, I'll get one of my colleagues to wire me up to the ERP...'

'The what?'

'Event related potentials.'

'I wish you guys had the same language as us. 'Factors influencing the course of the Franco-Prussian War' or something.'

'Some of us do. I don't do toys for the boys, do I? However...wires on my scalp, electrical activity in the brain...'

'And?'

'They show me a picture of you and I light up.'

He kisses the top of my head before getting more serious.

42.

'**M**iles'

'Hi. How're you doing?'

'Good thanks. I owe you some money.'

'Really? I thought we were all settled. Did I pay for something I don't know about?'

'No. I found fifty pence in our mother's purse.'

'You keep it. That can be your Christmas.'

I don't mention the card where she'd written down all the exams we'd passed. And the newspaper cutting from the time Elsa and I ran away. He always just found it funny.

'Dr Lamb? The Dean would like a word with you.'

Does this man not know how to use the phone?

'Dean. Madeleine Lamb here.'

'Madeleine. Nice to speak to you again. I was wondering whether you've made any progress?'

'I take it that you're referring to the Professor Mason thing?'

'Yes. And anything else you'd care to talk about, of course.'

'I'm no further forward, I'm afraid. Sorry.'

'Don't worry. It would have been nice to have had the whole thing done and dusted. I don't know if you've been told that we did have a word with Professor Mason?'

'Who's "we" if I may ask?'

'Myself and Desmond and Matthews, from Court.'

Court?

'University Court,' he says, as if he's heard my question.

I've been picturing Mason in the dock for too long.

'He didn't say to me. But then, he wouldn't, would he?'

'It was only a few days ago. I thought I'd leave it up to him to mention it. We didn't compel him. It's not part of his penance.'

He gives his little laugh. I envisage Mason lashing himself over the back with a cat's tail threaded with iron spikes.

'We always intended to keep you in the loop, Madeleine.'

Not to the extent of putting it in writing apparently.

'How about the young woman? Has she fully recovered?'

'Rosie?'

He knows and I know he knows.

'Yes, Rosie.'

'She seems fine at the moment.'

I stop myself from saying thank you.

'That's good. I'm glad there seems to be no lasting damage.'

So that it wouldn't be apparent in real court.

'I wouldn't be confident,' I say, 'about there being no lasting effects. Not when you lose a baby, not when you've had something like a psychotic breakdown, not when...'

'Young people are very resilient in my experience. I've got teenagers. I'm amazed at how they bounce back.'

Have they had their insides torn out? Their heads fucked with, their brains dowsed in chemicals and electric shocks? And oh, am I supposed to like him now because he has children?

'I'm just saying, personally I would consider her to be at risk for some considerable time.'

'At risk of what, Madeleine?'

'I couldn't possibly predict. I'm just trying to indicate the enormity of the experiences she's been through.'

'She's expecting another baby, I understand.'

'I'm surprised you know. I didn't think it was public knowledge.'

'We've been in touch with her family. We thought it advisable, you know.'

I can guess how they sought the advice.

'Then I'm surprised that the family told you.'

'Well that's the situation. It looks as if it's a good outcome all round really. I know it's not ideal, having a baby when you've just graduated, but if the university can be of help to her in any way with respect to her future career aspirations, then of course we would see it as our duty to do so. Our moral duty.'

I can read the subtext just as clearly as he can speak it.

'I fancy the pictures.'

I've been marking projects all day and the final call from the Dean has worn me out. Mel has improved sufficiently to be able to sit through a film.

'What do you fancy?' she asks.

'I want a diversion. Something funny. Something to make me feel good.'

It's not long – twenty minutes, in fact – before it becomes apparent that some error in judgement has occurred, on her part.

'Jesus god Mel.'

'Here.'

She shoves another paper hanky in my hand.

'Are you always like this?'

'I don't always sit through comedies – you said bloody comedy – where children are stolen from their mothers and have their eyes put out, where...'

'I'm sorry Maddie. I didn't know.'

'I know you didn't know. I'm sorry too. I'm not blaming you. Give me some more hankies.'

We draw in our feet to let the cleaner past. He ignores me.

'Do you think we can go home now?' Mel asks.

'In a minute.'

I cry all the way home in her car.

'Do you want me to come in?' she asks.

'No, no. Thanks Mel. I'm ok. I'll go to bed. I'll be better on my own.'

She pulls over in front of the flat. It's then I see Philip's car across the road. With him in it. He's not looking at us which is funny because I assume he's waiting for me.

'Damn.'

'Maddie?'

Mel looks shocked.

'I thought you'd be pleased to see him.'

'Yes I am. No. I'm not. I feel like being on my own. I told him I was going out with you tonight.'

'Don't let on. Just nip into your flat.'

'You think? I ought to speak to him. But it would hurt him if I told him to go. I can't stand that.'

'It would probably be less hurtful than running away from him.'

'But he won't know.'

I run up the stairs. My eyes are still cloudy with crying. I get the key in the lock.

Safe.

If this were someone else, I would say it was referred pain. What do I know though?

43.

'**D**o you think it would be worthwhile getting it published?'

'You mean, trying to get it published.'

'Yes.'

'Do you have a particular target in mind?'

'Psychologists, I thought.'

'I meant a journal that you might target. For publication.'

'Not really. I thought you might know some.'

'What were the main journals you were using in your write up?'

'I had about a hundred.'

'Are you not referring to articles rather than journals? Surely there were just a few main journals?'

'I don't remember.'

'It was a pre-load experiment, wasn't it? Restrained eaters?'

'Yes.'

'I've only read the draft of your introduction so far so I can't really say.'

'I got a significant result.'

'Just one?'

'Yes. It was highly significant.'

'Out of how many results, though? I'm trying to say, that's not really the way to judge something. You're right in a sense – they wouldn't publish a study if you didn't have any significant results. But the other question is, was it an important result?'

'It proved that there were differences between restrained

and non-restrained eaters.'

'I think people generally would agree there were differences between the two.'

A monkey would realise this.

'What specific differences?' I ask. 'Did they advance our theoretical understanding in any way?'

'I'll need to check. I had three pages on it in my discussion.'

'Why don't you do that? Have a look at the main journals you used and see whether you're making a contribution that's worth sharing.'

'It says in the Clinical Course Handbook that it helps to have a publication.'

'I'm sure that's true. It's helpful in many ways.'

My grandmother would have benefitted from a publication.

'There's a website in America where they totally publish undergraduate dissertations. You just send them in and they publish them.'

'They would need to be selective. Just think how many they would get from your class alone. Add in every Psychology Department in this country, then the USA, then...You get my point? Anyway, they would need to be cut down hugely on the size of the reports, do you not think?'

'They don't say so. The limit is 20,000 words.'

'How do you think it works then?'

'I don't know.'

'I think they're selling them on. That's what they'll be doing.'

'Do you really think so?' she says.

There are two more interruptions before I can eat my sandwich. Marjorie drops in to tell me that the External has passed the student in the Diploma class.

'You mean the one who failed?'

'I thought he was borderline myself and Jason seems to think it's ok.'

'That'll boost our pass rate nicely. What is it now? A hundred and ten per cent? Have we started passing people who aren't registered in the class yet?'

I shouldn't have mentioned the word 'registration' but she doesn't miss a beat.

'It's good for publicity,' she says, 'When the Dean goes out there on his recruitment drive it'll be very helpful.'

'For his long game of golf, you mean? Tell me, are they ever going to send any of their women over here? It's always men we get.'

'Maybe. The Dean is going to be negotiating something soon. He's got another visit lined up.'

Did Mason pause to tell he all this as they were entangled over the desk? Limbs scattering papers, sending the telephone flying across the room.

'There are going to be more distance learning arrangements,' she goes on. They won't need to come over here at all. We'll provide course outlines, train staff, authenticate their degrees.'

'Like a franchise.'

'You're far too cynical, you know.'

'Are you saying we're not in the commercial world? Don't we have "customers"?'

She ignores this.

'Can you not see the advantage? These women will participate in higher education for the first time. Supervised by Western academics.'

'In a research degree?'

'We go to them.'

'They don't let women out of the country so we're supposed to support that?'

'Not all of us.'

'What do you mean?'

'Just women members of staff. They won't allow male staff to supervise women. Do you not fancy a little trip yourself? All expenses etc.?'

There are many ways in which she and I are separated in our thinking. I wonder if she likes ice lollies or dogs even.

The next interruption is Charlie on the phone, to tell me that Rosie still can't email her Turnitin report because her laptop has crashed, possibly terminally. I get him to impress on her that it's urgent. I do wonder why she hasn't phoned herself.

The police are waiting at my door when I arrive home that night. They won't take coffee or tea.

'We've had a report of a disturbance at the back of your flat this afternoon. We've spoken to some of the neighbours already. There's been no actual break-in but a man was observed hanging around before trying to climb the scaffolding at the back. Fortunately one of your neighbours spotted him and scared him off.'

Bugger.

'It's always difficult when there's scaffolding up. We wanted to give you the description of the person concerned, though, in case he should been seen in the vicinity again. We're regarding it as an attempted burglary.'

'I hope so,' I say.

They look surprised and I explain about the phone calls.

'We've not got that here.'

I didn't expect that they would. I try to remember what the young man in the lecture looked like. The one who didn't know 'erogenous'. His difficulty was no doubt only semantic. But the intruder sounds nothing like my student, which is heartening: if erogenous boy is my stalker, at least he's not the one trying to gain entry to my flat.

44.

"Reminder. You were given advance notice of the randomly selected week you have been allocated for the Time Audit. Will you please complete this form promptly in order to avoid the need for further reminders? Time should be recorded as Teaching or Research and only if that is not possible should time be recorded as *Other*."

God bless the ragbag category. How many hours should I be seen to be working? Tony says Marjorie claimed seventy-five on her last one. How long for lunch? Am I allowed coffee breaks where I do no work, or do I always have to be reading an article or a book? Does something count as a journal if it's not high up on the citation index? What about non-peer reviewed journals?

Working seven hours a day seems reasonable. How, though, should I categorise listening to a colleague in tears about her man's betrayal? Phoning hospitals to check on missing students? Composing letters of discontent to the Administration? And what about thinking?

'You just go. That's fine, honestly.'

I pick up my glass and take a sip. Cold white wine at the end of a Friday. Philip takes hold of my hand.

'It's because I heard from Ryan and Vanessa,' he explains. 'They've only got another four weeks in Berlin and it's my last chance to go.'

'I don't mind. It'll let me get on with all this marking and I can go to Miles and Jen over Easter – I might stay over, in fact. It'll work out fine.'

'Are you sure you don't mind? I wish you would come

too.'

'It's not worth getting behind. You know what it's like. If you don't stick to your daily quota, it just gets hideous and stressful and you're up practically the whole night before handing back.'

'Couldn't you bring some with you?'

'Yes, right. You three swanning off to see the Wall or whatever, and me waving goodbye as I settle down to mark. Sorry. It would be too painful.'

'Are you sure you're not just making an excuse?'

'How? Why would I be doing that?'

'As a sort of avoidance.'

'Avoiding you? It doesn't look like that so far, does it?'

'No, but so far you've always had your own flat to retreat to whenever you felt like it. You've always been able to go out with your friends in between.'

'Of course. It's called life, isn't it?'

'Are you getting angry now?' he says.

'I wasn't but I could begin to.'

'Does that not suggest that there's some other agenda here?'

'Philip, there's nothing worse than having agendas attributed to you. You don't know my state of mind. Christ, we're the ones that are supposed to be able to do that and we can't. What hope does the French Department have? What is this great agenda of mine anyway?'

'Sometimes I get the feeling you're keeping yourself aloof. That you don't want to get drawn in too close.'

'What?'

'I'm guessing you're afraid of intimacy.'

'How long have we known each other? I mean, what's appropriate here?'

'A few months. But people can get close.'

'We are close though. Don't you like it the way it is?'

'I just worry that because I'm getting closer to you, you're getting afraid. I'm not sure what our relationship means.'

'Neither am I but I'm not going around asking myself. I prefer to let things unfold.'

'Don't you find it possible to predict?'

'Do you? What's happened with you in the past? Have you been able to predict?'

'Is that it? Have you been let down in the past when you've tried to make predictions?'

'Does one need to demonstrate a material base for all one's thinking? How Marxist. Here was me thinking you were being Freudian. I'm surprised at you. You're doing a lot of drawing inferences. You're meant to be a rationalist for goodness sake. You'll be talking star signs next.'

He laughs.

'Think about it, though,' he says. 'Is there not a grain of truth in it?'

'Philip, you're attributing a lot to me. A past I don't recognise, a latent content to what I say. Why don't you take it at face value?'

'There's never face value.'

'You might find it useful to pretend there is. The trouble with underlying structures is that there could be lots of different ones and who knows which would be right. Besides, I could equally well turn round to you and make up some story about how you're projecting your past on to me. How about that?'

'Go on then. Try.'

'All right. You are clearly sensitised to rejection. You see signs where they don't exist. You make impersonal things personal. This suggests to me that either you've been brought up in some precarious attachment mode – a thin but widespread rejection, let's say - which makes you generally insecure; or else, you've had a particular experience subsequent to childhood which has brought this about. Do you want me to go on?'

'Please.'

He takes a swig at his beer. Do I like his hands as well as I used to?

'What would this experience be then, beyond the

mothering one? A woman, obviously. Philip? A woman, not a man?'

'Not a man. No, never.'

'For the moment we won't look too closely at why you say 'never' when 'no' would have done. Remember you started this game. Ok. Someone you invested in – your love, of course. Someone who took that lightly and left you disappointed.'

'Who hasn't had that?'

'No-one. That's what I was going to say. This is all total shite, can't you see? And the same applies to your psychologising about me.'

'Your coat's fallen on the floor.'

He gestures to my side of the table.

'Are we agreed?' I go on. 'No more talk about this?'

'Maybe.'

45.

'**A**re you sure?'

She's very quiet.

'You know that it'll be more difficult next year, Rosie? You'll have the baby and god knows it'll be hard to combine that with studying.'

'I'll be living with Charlie. I'm going to be moving in soon.'

'The other thing is, there are likely to be changes in the courses. You would need to attend some of the classes again next year.'

'Could they not set a special exam?'

'That's not been the usual practice. Besides it's not just that courses might change. You were doing Dr Donaldson's option, weren't you?'

She nods.

'You see, he's retiring. There won't even be that option next year. What's changed, Rosie? Why are you talking about deferring now?'

'It's partly because of this Review thing. I don't have my computer back yet and...'

'If it comes to the bit, it's not going to count that much towards your final degree. We need to keep things in perspective. It's going to be much more important how you do in the exams.'

'That's another thing. I've not been feeling well. I've started to feel pretty squeamish and I nearly threw up yesterday.'

'How many weeks are you at now?'

'Ten.'

'Doesn't the sickness die down? Maybe you'll feel better by the time the exams start. You would get a medical certificate too, so that if the worst came to the worst in one of the exams...'

'I don't feel like it. My head is somewhere else. I've not been studying.'

'I'm sorry Rosie. I'm being stupid. It's like I've forgotten how much you've had to deal with. Plus the time off. I don't like bridges being burnt, that's all. There would be no harm in registering for the exams, then it would still be open to you to sit if things improved. When do you get your computer back? You could still hand in your review and the mark would stand next year. That would be something out of the way.'

'He promised it by yesterday but it wasn't ready when Charlie went in.'

'Chivvy the guy. Does he realise how important it is? We don't officially give extensions. I'm just relying on the Board allowing this to get through without any penalty.'

'I'll ask Charlie to talk to him,' she says.

It's difficult to believe she's growing a baby.

'She's still off.'

I've been trying to get hold of Susan the Rep.

'When is she coming back, do you know?'

'I think it'll be a while. As far as I understand, she's on long-term sick leave. But we don't get told the details. Quite right I suppose, but it makes things difficult.'

I wonder what hell she's going through. It's one thing to waken at five in the morning and groan at the thought of it all. But not to be able to get up, go out.

'Have you heard? She's putting herself forward for one of the teaching awards?'

'You're nuts.'

'I beg your pardon.'

I wonder for a minute if Tony is seriously offended.

'I think you mean that she's nuts.'

He's talking about Marjorie.

'I do. Of course I didn't mean you. But how can she? She only teaches the Diploma students. She's got twenty in the class. Compare that, if you will, with the two hundred and ninety-five that you and I have. And...'

'And she only does about ten lectures a year.'

'How did you know I was going to say that? I suppose she'll claim all the supervision. But that's different from stand-up stuff. What possible justification...what could she possibly have said about herself?'

'Or someone else. She needs a sponsor remember.'

'Mason. Of course. Legs up leg up. Chrissake would it not make you sick?'

'Apparently she's claiming that her feedback is better than everyone else's,'
Tony goes on.

'Number one, she shouldn't know about other people's feedback. It's meant to be personal and the only other... ah yes, Mason again. He's shown her I bet. Bastard.

'Number two, any idiot can give good lectures if they've only got ten to do in the year.'

'Do you think she'll get it?'

'If she's got his support, probably. Even if we just apply Sod's Law. It would be just like the thing.'

'How come you know all this stuff anyway?' I ask him. 'You're always telling me things. Who's your source? How come I don't give you any gossip?'

'But you do. The scanner and all that.'

'I suppose.'

I wonder.

46.

The secretary points to the phone.

'That's his mother,' she says. 'She spoke to him last night. He knew about the exam and wasn't too anxious. I don't think he's gone and topped himself or anything.'

She looks apologetic.

'I didn't say that to her,' she adds unnecessarily.

'So why is he not at the exam then?'

He's the only one missing out of a hundred and thirty.

'Who knows? He's not answering the landline or his mobile at the moment. Maybe he's still asleep. His mother's going to keep trying.'

'How far away does he live?'

She looks up his record on the screen.

'Not far. About ten minutes.'

'I wonder if we should send someone over?'

'Is that done? To go to their flats?'

'Frankly, Marilyn, I don't care. If it prevents all the complications of missing an exam...'

Her phone goes again.

'It's Jason,' she says, whispering.

He's in the exam hall, which is why the secretary is speaking softly.

'He says the student has just arrived.'

'Thank goodness. What's the story?'

'He's covered in sick. He's been throwing up half the night and only managed to get himself into a taxi about fifteen minutes ago.'

'Poor little sod. It's good he's managed to come in,

though. I'll go over and see what's what.'

You forget how anxious some of them get. You have to be in the exam room for a while before the smell of sweat begins register. When I get to the hall, the exam officer from Registry drops in, doing his rounds.

'How is it? Is everything all right?'

People in Registry worry in case the exam papers don't arrive in time. Indeed, how is it? I pause to think about the five Disability students who started the exam early. The other four who are sitting in separate rooms spread about the campus, two requiring computers, one a scribe and one a midwife. I think about the girl with ME who is allowed to take a sleep in the middle of the exam, and the student in the hall who has one leg propped up on a cushion after an injury.

'How is it?' I say to him. 'It's like fucking Lourdes, that's how it is.'

After an hour the balls of my feet are sore with tiptoeing around the hall. Don't write any more, I say under my breath: I have to read all this. I hope your pen dries up. This had better be relevant because I'm going to give you no marks unless it is, and on top of that you're going to make me so angry that even if it does end up being related to the question, I won't be in any frame of mind to appreciate it. So be very careful. And that's an awfully big cardigan you have on there, young lady, for such a small person. Do you have big wads of lecture notes tucked away that you pull out when I'm not looking? I'll turn round suddenly and catch you at it, see if I don't.

'Jason. Coffee break. Do you want to go first or what?'

He lets me go. Walking through the quad I think again about the gap there is in the exam. There's no empty place in the hall of course. We've known in advance and the janitors have set out the right number of desks. But there's no Rosie and it doesn't feel right.

At the end of the exam, before allowing them to leave, we stack the bundles of scripts into piles of ten, the better to count them. We get it wrong – the numbers don't tally with the attendance sheet. The students are getting restless and the noise is high. Phones are switched on, creating a cacophony. We count the piles again, finally packing them into black rubbish bags after the students are dismissed. We swing the bags over our backs and make our way to the Department where Marilyn will sort them out for the markers. The students have dispersed in clumps. They wouldn't like to see their work ending up in bags, like so many body parts.

On the grass outside the library, those with exams ahead are sprawled about, making the most of an early summer sun while idly leafing through their notes. The sun always shines in exam time, the pleasure of it sharpened by anxiety.

47.

Mel is sitting on the floor complaining about parents who all expect "A"s in Art.

'I can't believe how much work I'm having to do on these bloody portfolios.'

She stretches her legs.

'Don't you just want a dog?' she goes on.

I've never heard her say this before. Besides, it's a bit of a jump.

'What aspect appeals to you? Is it the early winter morning walks in the rain when you've got flu? What's come over you?'

'Just not to think about it. You would be living with someone – well, sort of someone - but not need to think about it. There would be no conflict. You provide the food. They love you.'

'You can't even make it home for your own dinner, far less a poor dog's. What if you stayed out for the night? I mean the whole night. You couldn't do that anymore, do you realise? Not without having arranged a dog-sitter.'

'That's it, then.'

'What? You're going to get a dog-sitter? You're *going* to be a dog sitter?'

'I'm never going to get a dog, that's what. It's funny how it can take just one thought to make up your mind.'

'I suppose you do your thinking in painting.'

'That's an insult, I take it?' she says.

'It's a compliment. I would love to be without words. Imagine, just paint.'

'I don't need to imagine and it's not like you think. It's

just as stressful.'

    'How's that nice new guy?'

    'Still nice.'

    'That's been a while. It must be all of weeks.'

    'Cheeky bitch. Eight weeks and two days.'

    'Can you not be a bit more precise?'

    'Come seven o'clock tonight.'

    'He's nice, Mel. I really liked him at the party.'

    'He's nice. He *is* nice.'

    'You make it sound like a sentence. From a judge.'

    'I don't mean boring nice. He's sort of quirky nice,' she says.

    'Like?'

I so hope it won't be along the lines of 'I'm such a zany person'.

    'He brought me a present the other night.'

    'Yes?'

    'It was a book.'

Good start, I think. But please don't let it be "Le Petit Prince".

    'Go on then.'

    'Kant's Critique of Pure Reason.'

The upcoming final year students are already looking for supervisors for their research projects next year: "I have always loved your area of psychology and it would be awesome if I could be supervised by you next year. I know you are a very popular supervisor so I hope I'm not too late." The flattery route.

    Some want to find the cure for schizophrenia. Or investigate depression in students. Good topic, I say, but it's already been heavily researched and it's difficult to imagine you could contribute anything new in this area. Eating disorders are a popular choice. "I could expose subjects to pictures from magazines and see how it affected their eating patterns." How would you operationalise this? I ask, and then hear nothing more. One lone student has outlined a specific proposal with three hypotheses listed and an attached link to a journal article. Top of the list.

'I don't know who to talk to. It's about my daughter. She's so upset at the timetable. She's got all her exams in two days. She's a joint student. She's got two exams for her other Department on the first day and then on the next, she's got three Psychology ones. They're saying it's only one exam but it's three topics. I just feel it's not fair. Not after all the work she's done over the years and for it all to land in two days. And the second day is a Saturday. She's in there till five o'clock. Who's at their desk at five o'clock? I can't understand that. I know it's not your fault. Someone else said it was the administration who do it and that you can't do anything about it. My daughter says, do you think they're going to change all the dates of the exams because of me, Mum? Well, I can see the sense of that but it's so unfair. Why should she be penalised? She's so conscientious, she's a real perfectionist. She would be mad if she knew I was phoning you. I'm really sorry about this. I know there isn't anything you can do but I just had to tell someone. I didn't really know who to speak to. She was waiting for the timetable to come out. It was so late. I've not slept since then, to be honest. Of course I try not to let it show. She just carries on. She's so good that way. I've got a son as well. They're different, girls. I just want it to be right for her, after all her hard work. She wasn't happy about her project too. It wasn't up to her high standard in the end but she put it in all the same. Well, she had to. She would have lost marks for being late, wouldn't she? She just said she would put all her effort into her exams and now it looks...'

She sniffs with tears.

'And now it looks as if she won't get the first she was hoping for. I said to her, it doesn't matter to us, dear, what you get so don't you worry about that. But we did think she would maybe get a first and now that's all spoiled. I don't know what to do.'

48.

'**C**an you see him?'
    The police are sitting in my flat, taking me through a large folder of photos.
'Look at this one.'
I don't recognise him at all.
'Your neighbours picked him out. He's the one from your garden. He's not one of your students then?'
    'He's not the one I sort of thought he might be.'
The one I'm faced with is thin faced, with the little bump and hollow at the top of the cheeks that says deprivation. A boy who's been brought up with no one ever worrying about him.
    'So maybe we've got two people here,' he suggests. 'This one is the intruder and then there's someone else who's been phoning you.'
    'I guess so.'
It would be nicer if it had been more simple – my caller being removed, even if just for trespassing.
    'When did he last call you?'
'A few nights ago. I put the phone down when he said my name.'
    'Are you sure it was the same one?'
How many stalkers do they think I have? Eventually they leave, giving me the feeling I was bad because I hadn't delivered.

The sun strikes off the steel tables outside the pub. I hear my name. It's the final year
students, three drinks into the afternoon of their exams ending.
    'Hey Maddie.'

They're more casual than ever, already seeing themselves as ex students. I, on the other hand, will sign myself Dr Lamb until after the Exam Board. One of the boys stands up and indicates his chair.

'Here. Have a seat, Maddie. What can I get you?'

'No no. I should be buying you one. You can get me a drink when you've got a job. Please. What would you like?'

I go round the table though they're reluctant. Can my memory cope with the names of drinks I've never heard of?

'Why don't you help me carry,' I say to the boy, thinking myself clever.

We go inside to the bar, me rehearsing the list. Two girls are standing there, holding drinks and talking loudly. They look familiar and the boy who's come with me hails them.

'I'm getting the drinks,' I say to them. 'What would you like?'

'We're fine thanks,' one of them says.

She holds up her glass to show it's half full.

'You'll be needing another one soon. What are you on?' I press her.

'No. It's ok,' she says.

'We're not even Psychology students,' says her friend. 'But thank you anyway.'

The boy carries the tray outside while I pay. When I go out, they're talking about a band I've never heard of. The sun is in my eyes and I have to shield them to see. It's getting hotter and I feel my tights sticking to my legs. I look at my watch surreptitiously. Two or three drinks is a mile ahead and I've no intention of catching up.

'Hey, sorry guys.'

This comes out as more informal than I intended.

'I'll need to go. I'm just down this way to get some things from the Asian shop. I'm cooking for a friend so I'll need to be off. But have a good time.'

I mean it.

Philip turns up early when I'm still preparing the food. I've not had a chance to change and feel self-conscious and scruffy. He puts the wine in the fridge, starts to set out cutlery on the table. I look at the back of him. How can people live together? You just manage to extricate yourself from your mother and father when you're expected to share your life with someone who will disturb the books on your shelves in a way that your parents never did.

'I'm afraid I'll need to do some marking later, Philip.'

'That's ok. I've got some too. We can mark together if you like.'

But I like to eat apples and bite my nails when I'm marking, and besides I don't think I want anyone doing an audit on my work-distraction ratio.

'Can you wash that basil please?'

He's so obliging. Do I just like bad boys?

'I was thinking about the summer,' he starts, not looking at me but drying the leaves on some kitchen towel.

'Yes?' I say, looking in the cupboard for plates.

'What about South America? Or Cuba? You've said you fancy Cuba.'

'I do. I'd like to go but I'm not sure about this year.'

There's a short silence.

'Really? But you want a holiday surely?'

'I feel as if I need one. I don't think I've quite...well, my mother's death. I know she and I weren't best friends but still. It's been a big change.'

'So why not Cuba now?'

'I'm not sure I can afford it this year.'

'Honestly? I thought...'

'My mother's money? It's not settled yet. Miles is still having meetings with the lawyer. It's doubtful whether anything will come through before the summer at this rate. It's very complicated you know.'

I regret saying this.

'I do know.'

He stares at me.

'I can lend you money if you like?'

'Thanks. That's really good of you. But I don't want to be indebted.'

'It wouldn't be for long.'

'It would still make me feel uncomfortable. What if I died on the trip? You would never get your money back.'

'Jesus Christ Maddie. What a thing to say. If you died on the trip, money would be the last thing on my mind.'

'It's just a thing I've got. I like to be independent.'

'Do you really? Or do you mean, independent of me?'

'How could I tell?'

'Well, did you have the same desire to be independent when you've been with other guys? Let me put it another way. Have you allowed yourself to be dependent with any other guy?'

'I'd need to think about it. Can you switch that oven off please while you're there.'

'You're trying to avoid this conversation.'

'Because I asked you to switch off the oven?'

'Frankly, yes.'

'I don't know what I'm doing. I've said to you before, I'm not ready to commit.'

'Going on holiday, as I've said before, is not commitment. It's a holiday.'

'It doesn't feel like that. I can't help it.'

'I think it's like I said. You're worried about committing to me because underneath you're really worried about my commitment to you.'

'And I've said I don't think that's right.'

'I could make it easier. I can give you an assurance about my commitment.'

'I don't think that would help.'

'Madeleine…'

My Sunday name. I'm in trouble

'Come here. Look at me.'

I walk over meekly.

'What's the matter?' he asks.

He puts his arms round me.

'I'm beginning to feel a bit…I don't know,' I start to try to explain. 'Hemmed in, sort of.'

"Trapped" is the word I'm avoiding.

'It's difficult to explain,' I go on. 'But see when I'd come back after being out with Mel and you were waiting in the car across the road from the flat. I saw you. I know I didn't say at the time. I probably should have. It made me feel…'

The usual tactic of watering down the criticism, putting the blame or focus on oneself.

'Why the hell didn't you say? You see, that's what I mean about you. Anyone in their right mind would just have said to me.'

'Do you think?'

'I know so. You're not the first woman I've been out with, you know.'

'There's no need to remind me.'

'What have you heard? Did Martin say anything to you while the pair of you were canoodling next door?'

The night of the perfect dinner party.

'I was not canoodling, as you call it. Your friend has a lot to answer for though.'

'What does that mean?'

'Do you think it's ok to make passes to your friend's girlfriend?'

'So he did?'

'I would say he did. It wasn't reciprocated, needless to say.'

'What did he say about me and previous women, then?'

'Not a lot. Just that it had been a bad breakup with the last one.'

'Shall I tell you? I can tell you how bad it was.'

'Philip, thank you but really I don't want to know. Maybe you're so worried about making the same mistake again that you end up making a different one.'

'Do you realise how difficult you're being?'

'In not wanting you to tell me about your past?'

'In avoiding talking about our future.'

'We've been through this before. The last time. We agreed to leave things as they are. To just let things develop.'

'How can they develop if you won't see me?'

'I do see you. I am seeing you now.'

'Like you would see the postman or the joiner. We are in the same place at the same time.'

'That's not fair. We're much more than that and you know it.'

'So what about the holiday? What am I supposed to do?'

'You could always fix up something...'

'Like at Easter? Go on my own?'

'I don't know what else.'

'If you are worried about me, Maddie, about my intentions, if it helps...why don't we just get married?'

'What? Are you off your head? Oh sorry, sorry.'

I see the look on his face.

'I didn't mean that, honest. That wasn't very nice of me. What I meant was, it doesn't seem very rational.'

'As you can see, I'm not feeling very rational. This whole thing has got me quite upset. Honest to god I just asked you to commit yourself to one lousy holiday and now look where we are.'

He takes a swig of wine from the glass he pours himself.

'Me too.'

'What? Oh. Wine. Sure. I'm sorry.'

'I won't say cheers,' I say, gulping it down.

I need all the chemical help I can get.

'I don't feel like eating,' he says, putting his glass on the table. 'I think I'll get back and start on my marking.'

'Sure. Sorry.'

'What for?'

'For everything.'

'Don't be silly. I'm sorry too. Maybe more than you know.'

I hate threats like that.

'I'll phone you tomorrow. Don't work too hard. Get a good sleep.'

He kisses me on the cheek and lets himself out the front door.

49.

'I'm going over now. I'll see you when you come.'

Mel has just broken the news on Marcia's behalf. We're all going to meet at Louisa's flat. Marcia has broken up with her husband.

'I don't know who instigated it,' Mel says on the phone. 'It might even have been mutual. Things haven't been good for a while, as we know.'

'That sounds like a lot of marriages,' I say.

Marcia is not one to open her heart, especially when there's more than one person present and she's sober. It shows the severity of it all.

'You don't need to say, Marcia, about why. Just tell us how you're feeling though.'

Louisa pats her on the shoulder the way you would a child.

'It's ok. I don't mind talking about why. I feel like shit but then you could have predicted that. I still don't know if it's going to stick. I wouldn't be surprised if we just went back to old habits. It's so much easier staying married, isn't it?'

'How would we know?' Mel asks.

'Because it's the same as having a relationship but worse. The habit is more ingrained and besides there's all the work of disentangling. Dividing things up. I just dread that. Don't ever do it girls, that's all I can say.'

She starts to cry.

'Some of us just wish we had the chance,' says Mel.

'I don't know so much,' I say.

Louisa is quiet.

'I'll tell you from the beginning,' says Marcia. 'But nothing about sex though. Some things are private.'

Thank Christ for that.

By the end of the evening we're all giggling, totally drunk. It's four in the morning before I get to bed. Louisa and I have walked part way home together, arm in arm.

'We'll feel this tomorrow.'

My head is sore already but from trying not to cry.

'I know I know. You would think we'd learn, wouldn't you?'

'Poor Marcia,' I say.

'She's better off without him.'

'She won't feel that though.'

'No. Not for a long time.'

'It's really sad.'

I begin to feel really, really sad.

'Do you think I'm stupid then?' she asks.

'What? Why would I think you were stupid? Where did that come from?'

'I was going to tell you. Before all this happened.'

'What?'

'I think I'm getting married.'

'What? You and Mike?'

'Who else?'

'Wow. Louie.'

I stop to give her a hug.

'I'm really pleased for you. It's great. He seems really nice. I thought he was really nice. You mustn't let this put you off. Marcia and thing.'

I can't even remember her husband's name now. And I sound ten years older than Lou. I sound like her mother. The thought makes me cry again.

'I'm sorry Louie. I'm really happy for you. I'm not crying about that. It's just all too much. Things are too big. Do you know what I mean? Big.'

'Yes. Well no. I mean I don't care. Whatever you say. Come on I think we're going in the wrong direction.'

I'm flying, I'm horizontal. The dance is wild, my arms are locked with Tony who has another woman on the other side and I'm flying. You think about what bits of clothing might be lost.

Philip and I have arrived late. A large group of glamorous young things is being lined up by a photographer on the stairs. How can there be so many? One or two wave to me. Of course, the students, scrubbed up. My goodness, they're grown up and lovely. Even their parents might think so.

The staff are invited to join a class photograph and I leave Philip, to stand near the back of the group with my arms over the shoulders of two girls. Throughout the evening, students come up and get their photo taken with the staff, who've ganged up at the same table. It's difficult to think that I won't see my project students again, after being close all year. They'll send two or three emails asking a reference; one of them might keep in touch for two or three years but then they too will vanish from my screen and my head, making room for new people.

Mason is sitting opposite me, his wife on my left-hand side.

'It should really be boy, girl, boy, girl, shouldn't it?' she says.

Is this the perfect family? Four children seems a bit unnecessary.

'You're from French, I believe, is that right?' she says, leaning over me and addressing Philip. I can smell her perfume, feel the heat from her skin.

'You've done your homework,' he laughs.

'Roo keeps me up to date on everything,' she says.

Does she use this pet name when talking to the Vice-Chancellor about him?

'Do you go to France regularly, Philip? I would think you need to keep up your language skills.'

'I've got friends there. Mind you, we don't do much

language teaching in my department now.'

'Really? How's that?'

'There's more emphasis on culture and literature. A lot of students have a poor grasp of the language when they come in so it's more like remedial French. It's combined with general courses on the history, art and literature of France, of course.'

'How interesting,' she says.

Such a serviceable word.

'It's the same in Classics,' Philip goes on. 'There's very little teaching of Latin proper. Just Latin for tourists, sort of thing. Greco-Roman culture. But then, I'm sure you know what it's like in the university these days.'

'Roo is very against the dumbing down idea,' she says quickly.

'Good for him,' says Philip.

I try to reconcile this with the Mason I know.

'He's adamant that it isn't happening,' she says. 'He says that students are far better taught now and that's why they're getting better degrees.'

'What about the French classwork nowadays?' I say. 'They just do an outline for an essay instead of the full thing.'

'I don't know anything about that, I'm afraid.'

The sequins on her dress are giving me a headache. On the other hand, Philip is looking particularly attractive. Perhaps because he's an ally at the moment. By the time Mason comes to give his speech, I almost don't care about the matey tone he adopts. The students laugh and applaud loudly when he tells a self-deprecating anecdote. I, on the other hand, know it's just his social skills ratcheted up a notch.

The next day, being generally incapable, I engage in the pseudo work of reading journals which need to be monitored but have no pressing relevance. This gives me an impression of making progress. My other pastime involves checking lecture feedback on the portal. Anonymous feedback. The Director of Teaching tells us that overall it was felt that the standard of teaching had dropped on account of "particular problems relating to foreign accents, grammar and mumbling". For my own part, can there really be four students who've made the identical comment: "Madeleine tries hard but..."? The vagaries of IT surely? Finger held on the submit key too long? But can't they just be straightforwardly vicious without patronising me to boot? In the main, what they say is positive and resonates with the warmth they show when they pass by on their way out of lectures. Complaints that are impersonal – only "57% for availability of references in the library" – are easily negotiated but ones closer to home have a potency, creeping into your mind for days like an overused tune.

I'm relieved by a call from Mel.

'Are you alone?'

Her voice is starched.

'Can you talk?' she goes on.

'Yes. I'm on my own. I'm just pretending to work. Are you at school? I can't hear the usual pandemonium.'

'No. I'm out. I've been at the hospital.'

'What? Not A and E? Is it your injury again?'

'It's not Brazilian. It might be something serious.'

She goes on to explain about a lump.

'Why didn't you say? I would have gone with you.'

'I know you guys think I'm just a straight extravert but I don't like to talk about things like this. At least, not until I know what's going on.'

'So what did the hospital say? Who did you see?'

'The Head Boy himself. He was very sweet, I have to say. Well, patronising actually, but who cares when your life is in their hands?'

'What happened?'

'He thinks it's probably a cyst and he tried to aspirate it but it was too difficult. He couldn't do it properly. So I got a mammogram done. They gave me the results to take back to him. He says he's reassured by what he saw though he scared the life out of me by calling in other doctors to have a look. I ended up with four of them crowding round the screen. Thoughtless bastards.'

'But it looks good Mel.'

'It's not conclusive, you know. I've got to go back in a couple of months to see whether there's any change.'

'But still. It's better than it could have been.'

There's such a desire to say something hopeful.

'I'll appreciate my life now,' she says. 'Grim Reaper Therapy.'

'No you won't. You'll love every breath of it for a day and then the usual hell will come back.'

'Sod off.'

50.

They're chattering like it's a Sunday School trip.

'May we begin now? Thank you for coming, first of all.'

I'm looking round, noting those who are absent either by lateness or intent. Those who are here are still talking, clattering their coffee cups. I pause and let them feel the silence. Mason is the last to subside.

'Thank you for coming,' I repeat, 'and may I welcome our External Examiner, Professor Parton. Good to have you back Anne,' I say, turning to her. She smiles at the assembly who are now quiet.

'Are there any apologies?'

Marilyn, sitting on my other side, takes notes.

'Before we begin the business of the meeting, I would just like to record my thanks to the people who have worked so hard to get us to this point. Apart from us doing the marking, that is. Marilyn has put an enormous amount of effort in preparing the papers for today and as always I am extremely grateful to her.'

Marilyn writes this down. I go on to thank others before reminding them of the confidentiality of the proceedings.

'You can take the papers away but please take care to keep them under lock and key,' I end up.

This is the nearest I get to being a spy.

'As you know, we have to log all relevant medical evidence and I'll do that with each case in turn but first of all we need to record the case of one student who has asked to defer her exams until next year. This is student 103 at the top of your list. To remind you, at the Preliminary Meeting we agreed this concession on the grounds of the difficulties that the student experienced during the course of the year. Anne has now ratified this as External so the deferment can be confirmed.'

My high heels are killing me already.

'I've also advised Anne about the penalties we decided on last week in relation to late work and she is fully in agreement. And finally, I have shown her our report on the moderating process and it is acceptable to her, is that right Anne?'

Anne murmurs beside me.

'So can we turn now to the business of deciding on degree class for each student? As you know, Anne has seen our proposed firsts and has looked at all the borderline cases. I'll ask her to speak to each of these when we come to them. Let's begin - candidate 74 first of all.'

Number 103. Rosie.

Two hours have gone by and the room is steaming up. Someone opened the windows earlier but they had to be shut again because of the traffic noise from outside. Anne has been presenting painstaking evidence about borderline cases and we've wrangled over criteria to use: mode instead of mean; exit velocity. In some instances, plain humanity.

'What about a short break?' she suggests.

She and I continue the discussion about lack of guidelines for the discretionary zone. I don't feel refreshed afterwards. At the end of the break it's like herding sheep back into place as they fetch cold coffee and grab the remaining biscuits, the muffins being finished. Near the end of the meeting, before representatives arrive from other Departments to decide on joint students, I invite people to raise general issues. Mason is in first.

'I have been conducting discussions with the Dean and members of the University Standards Committee,' he opens.

This is news to me.

'There is a general proposal to modify the process of calculating the final grades of honours students. I want to stress that this does not affect first- and second-year students. What I say is still at the level of debate but Heads of Department have been asked to raise the matter in an appropriate forum so that staff views might be solicited.'

Why didn't the bugger put it on the agenda?

'You don't mind, Madeleine, if I hijack the meeting for a few minutes?'

He says this without looking at me.

'Students at the moment have sixteen components all of which contribute equally to their final grade. This has the merit of being straightforward. I also appreciate the fact that we now deal in numbers. I can remember discussions with Philosophy when they were still insisting on 'beta double plus with a hint of minus' kind of stuff.'

Everyone laughs. I might have found it funny coming from someone else. Like myself.

'At higher levels,' he goes on, explaining to us piglets, 'is a rather novel proposal. As you know, there is a concern about numbers. Not in Psychology – we're holding up rather well, but in the university as a whole the entry rates and attrition rates are worrying. There are considerable financial implications of course. It has been suggested, accordingly, that as a way of making us more attractive as a university, both for first choice and for encouraging a sustainability of numbers...'

The heads have started to lower. Someone is picking bits of chocolate chip out of their biscuit.

'...that we should introduce a new heuristic. That we should recognise that it's expecting too much from students that they perform optimally across all the topics that they have to master – and make no error, they have to get on top of much more information than they ever did in the past – that in order to achieve this, we should make allowances for a slightly poorer performance in some area.'

I'm having trouble following. I'm feeling too old for subordinate clauses.

'So what does this mean?' I ask. 'Specifically.'

The heads lift up.

'Specifically, there is a proposal on the table – I won't say where it emanates from –that in future we operate a policy of disregarding the four worst components of a student's performance.'

'Out of sixteen?'

'Yes.'

'We let them fail a quarter of the exam? And they could still get a first, you mean?'

'The spirit of the proposal is that we focus on the merits of our students, not their weaknesses. It's realistic, after all, to condone a little – let me not say 'failure' – a little...'

'Softening of their performance,' Marjorie chips in.

'Softening. That's a good way of putting it.'

'I trust they're not applying this to the medics?' asks Tony. 'I don't fancy my GP suffering from "a bit of softness". Thank god we don't train pilots,' he adds.

'That's quite different. You're being provocative Tony,' says Mason. 'We sample depth in our final year. Depth. Breadth gets dealt with in first and second year. Now we are adding depth.'

Like layers to a wedding cake? Or are we talking pyramid selling now? My head is splintering.

'I wonder if we might ask the External for her views,' I suggest. 'Would you mind speaking to this, Anne?'

Her department, it transpires, has rejected such a scheme.

'Thank you, Anne,' Mason takes over. 'It's good to get your judgement but of course we will have to consult the new External when he takes over next year. I believe I'm right in saying that this is your last year with us?'

'I'm afraid we'll have to bring the discussion to a close now.'

I raise my voice since the room has split into smaller groups arguing noisily. When the joint departments arrive it's only Business Studies who pose any challenge, quoting rules to substantiate their case for giving their student a first.

They speak with such authority that you would think these regulations existed in stone. But I've looked them up. I know fine well that the certainty abides only in their heads.

It's ten to six when I usher in the representatives for our last meeting.

'This is Philosophy,' I say, 'in case you can't tell from looking at them.'

'You've lost it,' says Marilyn sitting next to me. 'You've lost it.'

51.

'Look at all the dogs. What's going on?'

There's line of people coming into the Estate, pulled by numerous dogs.

'It'll be the Doggy Dawdle,' I say.

'What?'

Philip has never heard of it. But then he hardly ever comes out here.

'It's a bit early in the day, is it not?' he asks.

White dew still sits on cobwebs in the rhododendrons.

'I suppose they figure that dog owners get up early. I guess it would be too busy later on, with cricket matches and what not.'

One dog has unwisely been let off the leash and is not fulfilling expectations. Why do owners ever think they might?

'Let's go down to the lake,' I suggest. 'We can cut across the field. They'll have to stick to the track.'

It's over the old bridge and further on down a hollow that we come across the scene. The police cordon hadn't been visible from the track, but they're already putting up a tent and staking out further territory with plastic tape signifying crime scene.

'What do you think?' I ask.

I feel uneasy.

'It's got to be trouble. They're not checking fish stock, put it that way'.

We've stopped.

'But the river is so shallow,' I say.

It bubbles over the rocks, creating light foam, small eddies. I can see it even from a distance.

'You're thinking the same as me,' he says. 'Look, I'll go down and ask. Do you want to wait?'

I nod, feeling my lips white. He moves slowly down the hill. One of the policemen comes up to meet him, to prevent him from going further. They're too far away for me to hear. My head has moved into a litany, a hangover from childhood. The rhythm masks the thoughts for a bit. Finally he turns and comes back up. His head is down. I don't go towards him but wait. He just looks at me for a minute.

'Please. Tell me.'

'I can't. They're not giving out much. I think it might have been a body, covered up.'

'That's not possible. Look at the river.'

'It must have come from further up.'

'It couldn't be washed down those shallows.'

I know I'm avoiding the point.

'Something was found by security staff this morning.'

I cover my mouth with my hands. Why didn't she just run away?

52.

In the Robing Room, I set the mortar on my head and adjust my gown. There's no mirror. I chat to my partner. It's like being paired off for an outing in primary school. Across the landing in the hall, we hear the organist coaching the assembly in their song. When finally the doors are opened for us to start the procession, the sense of excitement is palpable. Chattering students, best dressed mothers and fathers, the odd grey grandparent. The Hall looks like a large Battenberg cake, with gold pillars, roses and Fleur de Lys motifs.

The Vice-Chancellor slowly leads us down the middle aisle and heads turn to stare as the organ bellows out from the balcony. Everyone sings with heart: *Gaudeamus Igitur*. The building will surely burst. *Gaudeamus Igitur, juvenes dum sumus.*

> *Let us rejoice therefore, while we are young.*
> *After a pleasant youth*
> *After a troublesome old age*
> *The earth will have us.*

The last verse is never sung of course:

> *Let sadness perish!*
> *Let haters perish!*
> *Let the devil perish!*
> *Let whoever is against our school*
> *Who laughs at it, perish!*

After the ceremony, everyone crowds into the cloisters to take a glass of champagne. Students cross on to the grass in the quadrangle to be photographed, trees in the background, with their friends, parents, tutors. The sun is shining and life burns.

I feel a touch.

'Madeleine!'

It's the Dean. He pulls me into the group which includes Mason and his wife as well as the Vice Chancellor.

'You know Desmond, don't you Madeleine? Here, let me introduce you.'

The Vice-Chancellor shakes my hand, looking at me briefly.

'I was telling the Vice-Chancellor how much you have to celebrate,' the Dean goes on.

'Me?'

'Your department.'

'Ah.'

'You may not have heard. This is hot off the press.'

He smiles.

'First of all, Marjorie Sweet has won the teaching award. The national one, that is, not our own little hand-knitted one. Did you know?'

'I heard about it.'

'It's wonderful. We're expecting the Press. Look, she's over there with her graduates.'

So she is. Face flushed. In the centre of a dozen young men laughing to the camera. Mason and his wife have their back to her.

'Was there something else you were referring to?' I ask.

'Indeed. Robin here' - he gestures to Mason- 'has just been confirmed in a highly prestigious post in Sierra Leone. He's going to be responsible for setting up the first Cognitive Neuro-Imaging Centre in Northern Africa. It's a tremendous opportunity to do pioneering work.'

I see. No culture of ethical requirements then. Just like novice surgeons getting posts in developing countries.

'We'll miss him,' the Dean goes on. 'He'll be a big loss to the Department, won't he? But he'll be back. It's only a two-year posting.'

Mason is listening silently. His wife has engaged someone

on her other side.

'Sorry Dean. You'll need to excuse me. I can see my friend there.'

I have trouble pushing my way through the crowds in the quadrangle.

'Maddie!'

The Dean has come after me. He lowers his head closer to mine.

'I just wanted to say – thank you very much for not taking that matter any further. No really...'

I was about to say something.

'It hasn't gone unnoticed, don't worry. It would have crucified him, you know,' he explains. 'We've only got our humanity after all, haven't we?'

He presses my arm and turns away.

I go back to my office and make a phone call. The answering voice is metallic and in my mind I see a woman with a titanium headdress and long nails painted silver:

'Marcombe Legal Associates,' she says. 'How may I help you?'

'This is a Doctor Lamb speaking. Madeleine Lamb. I'd like to make an appointment.'

Let the battle begin.

On my way home I pass a man handing out leaflets. He's well dressed and middle-aged.

'Are you a believer?' he asks, as I mindlessly accept one of his religious tracts.

'No,' I say.

'This is especially for you then,' he calls after me. 'God bless you.'

I stop and turn back to him.

'Nothing is deserved, you know. You need to know that. Nothing is deserved.'

Further down the road I put the leaflet in a bin.

THE END.

ABOUT THE AUTHOR

Gillian M Mayes

Gillian Mayes is an academic, now with honorary status. The background to this book, a campus novel, is thus well known to her. After retiring she went over to the other side and became a student in creative writing. But she'd always written a lot before that, starting with diaries at age eleven. These had to be abandoned when her children learned to read. She's had a lot of short stories published. A novel is something else, akin to crossing the Sahara, she says.

Printed in Great Britain
by Amazon